DEATH DUES

Recent Titles by Geraldine Evans from Severn House

The Rafferty and Llewellyn Mysteries

DYING FOR YOU
ABSOLUTE POISON
BAD BLOOD
LOVE LIES BLEEDING
BLOOD ON THE BONES
A THRUST TO THE VITALS

The Casey and Catt Mysteries

UP IN FLAMES
A KILLING KARMA

DEATH DUES

A Rafferty & Llewellyn Mystery

Geraldine Evans

This first world edition published 2008
in Great Britain and the USA by
SEVERN HOUSE PUBLISHERS LTD of
9–15 High Street, Sutton, Surrey, England, SM1 1DF.

British Library Cataloguing in Publication Data

Evans, Geraldine
  Death dues. - (A Rafferty and Llewellyn mystery)
  1. Rafferty, Joseph (Fictitious character) - Fiction
  2. Llewellyn, Sergeant (Fictitious character) - Fiction
  3. Police - Great Britain - Fiction 4. Detective and
  mystery stories
  I. Title
  823.9'14[F]

  ISBN-13: 978-0-7278-6647-9   (cased)

All Severn House titles are printed on acid-free paper.

Typeset by Palimpsest Book Production Ltd.,
Grangemouth, Stirlingshire, Scotland.
Printed and bound in Great Britain by
MPG Books Ltd., Bodmin, Cornwall.

Megan, this one's for you, in thanks for all your hard work in editing my typescripts.

Prologue

Joseph Rafferty riffled through the pages of quotations for caterers and photographers, florists and all the rest, thought, Why do weddings have to cost so much? – and said, 'I can feel my credit cards wincing from here and they're all the way across the hall.' And he hadn't even looked at the honeymoon holiday brochures yet.

He'd proposed to Abra just before Christmas the previous year. Much to his astonishment, she'd said yes. Then, it had been all hearts and roses and romance. But now the cold reality of modern weddings and their expense hit him in the face with all the force of a frozen kipper. Why they had to go through all this rigmarole . . .

'Don't be such a tightwad, Joe,' his fiancée complained. 'I don't want a hole in the corner wedding. People will say we've something to hide.'

'And if we fork out for what this lot are charging –' he picked up a stack of quotations and let them drop back to the table amongst the breakfast dishes – 'we *will* have something to hide. Ourselves. From the friendly, neighbourhood bailiffs.'

Abra tossed her long, chestnut hair and gave him a poke in the ribs as she said with a challenging air, 'Aren't I worth it, then?'

This, of course, put Rafferty in a cleft stick. Damned if he said yes and damned if he didn't. 'Of course you're worth it, my little Peach Melba. But you must remember I'm not Rockerfeller. I'm just a humble cop still paying for all the new stuff we bought for the flat.'

'And that's another thing. I think we ought to sell this place and buy a house.'

'But we've only just decorated throughout!' he protested. 'Not to mention all the new furniture we've bought.'

'Exactly. That's the most sensible time to sell. When the flat's looking its best.'

'I'd rather like to enjoy it looking its best myself. Anyway, I thought we were meant to be discussing the wedding, not moving home. Surely getting married is enough of a big thing to be doing at one time?'

'Maybe. But the flat's not mine and never will be. I'd like us to have a completely fresh start, when we begin married life. With a place that's *ours*.'

'We still haven't even settled on a date for the wedding,' Rafferty pointed out. Never mind *where*, which was likely to be another bone of contention.

'I thought next May.'

Rafferty nodded quickly. 'Next May's fine with me.' He was just glad to have got one thing sorted.

On that happy note, he stood and picked up his jacket. 'And now I've got to get to work.' And earn the money to pay for it all.

The wedding costs were getting seriously out of hand. Abra seemed to think she had to emulate the pomp of Lady Diana Spencer's wedding. And look how *that* marriage had turned out. All his attempts to encourage her to be reasonable had fallen on ears that were seemingly stuffed with cotton wool. It was as if she was bewitched by some mischievous wedding sprite and he didn't have the formula to break the spell.

Abra shuffled the wedding quotes into a neat pile. 'I'm off today so leave these to me. I'll make a start whittling them down. Some of them are charging way over the odds,' she conceded. 'I'll ring around and see if I can't knock them down a bit.'

A lot would be better, Rafferty thought as he kissed Abra goodbye, shrugged into his jacket and made for the door, picking up his raincoat on the way. But it was a thought he kept to himself. It wouldn't go down well and would only bring them back to Abra's 'Aren't I worth it?' argument, to which he knew he'd never find a winning response. 'I just hope this marriage does better than my first,' he muttered as he shut the front door behind him and made for the car.

One

The weather was blowing a gale. It blew through Rafferty's hair until it was pointing every which way. It picked up the sides and hem of his raincoat till it danced seemingly with a life of its own. As he rushed through the rain for the car, trying to restrain the whirling dervish antics of his raincoat, he just hoped nobody got themselves murdered today. He didn't fancy hanging around street corners in a downpour, the idle moments filled with musings on the type of house Abra might fancy in place of the flat. He hoped she hadn't meant it and had only said it to wind him up. The last thing he needed along with all the wedding expenses was to have the cost of moving to contend with. It wasn't as if the flat wasn't big enough. With three bedrooms, it could easily house a family. If she was serious, he would have to dissuade her from it. He could only hope he had more luck with that than he was having with the spiralling wedding costs. She might be trying to emulate Princess Diana's fairy-tale wedding, but he, no more than Prince Charles had been, was no Prince Charming. He also lacked the princely income.

He drove through the lashing rain from his home through the streets of Elmhurst, an attractive Essex town which even the grey day couldn't make ugly, to the police station's back entrance in Bacon Lane. The car park was full; even the super had beaten him in, he saw, as he took in his shining, top of the range Lexus, parked in the bay nearest to the station's rear entrance, a space sanctified as his by God and the superintendent. Rafferty had once or twice trespassed on its holy space and been soundly rebuked for his presumption.

He opened the door to the station's rear entrance and

dripped his way up the concrete stairs, depositing little droplets to catch the unwary with each squelching step upward. He could only hope the sainted super had reason to come down again shortly and slip and injure his fat arse and his dignity on the Rafferty-dropped rainwater. He should be so lucky.

He walked along the second-floor corridor to his office, wringing out his hair and his raincoat as he went and wishing, in spite of the wedding arrangements that Abra would, even now, be in the midst of organizing, that he was still at home and in bed with her, her let-down hair and silky nightie. He quelled the thought of this appealing prospect as inappropriate to the beginning of another working day and opened the door to his office.

His sergeant, Dafyd Llewellyn, had beaten him in as usual. He was sitting in the corner in Rafferty's office looking as neat as his desk and very industrious. Also as usual. After fighting his way through the wind and rain across the car park, Rafferty felt like something the cat had dragged in. He smiled to himself as he realized that, like Llewellyn, he too was a good match for his desk. He smoothed his unruly auburn hair into some sort of order and sat down behind the towering piles of files and other impedimenta to a well-ordered day. 'So what have we got, Dafyd?' he asked. 'Anything new come in?'

'No,' Llewellyn replied evenly. 'Unless, of course, there are any further muggings, it looks as if we'll have a quiet day.'

'Less of the fate-tempting, if you please.'

'Oh, and there's still that report on your desk that Superintendent Bradley wants you to read and initial.' Llewellyn's voice had the slightest tinge of disapproval as he added, 'It's been there nearly a week.'

Rafferty, hearing the disapproval, pulled a face and said, 'I suppose you've read it?'

Llewellyn nodded.

'Give me the condensed version, then. You know how wordy these bloody reports are. Not the way for a man to start the day by ploughing through a load of bumf.'

Llewellyn proceeded to explain the report. But since he

proved almost as wordy as the report itself, Rafferty stopped
him when he got to Section 3 Subsection iv c. 'That's enough.
Just nod if the powers that be are ordering yet another meeting
on the subject to discuss their preliminary findings.'

Llewellyn nodded.

'Thought so. Meetings and yet more meetings. It's a
wonder we ever get time to solve any crimes at all. I'll just
initial it. They'll still be meeting to discuss it come Doomsday.
Anything else?'

'The superintendent said for you to pop in to see him if
you're not too busy.'

Rafferty groaned. 'What's he want? Not to discuss this
with me, I hope.' He thumped the weighty report in disgust.

Llewellyn's lips twitched slightly. 'No. I think not. I understood him to say that he wishes to discuss the problem with
the local moneylenders. As you know, two of their collectors
were mugged last week.'

'And he wants to know what I'm doing about it, I
suppose?' Truth was, he wasn't doing a lot. Some if not
most of the local loan sharks' collectors were no more than
thugs adept at putting the frighteners on little old ladies
who got behind with their payments. Mugging was too good
for such people. 'Put a few grand sounding phrases together
for me, Daff. You know I'm no good at that. Something
that'll impress the super. You know the sort of thing.
Sentences with lots of words and loads of PC bollocks.
He'll like that.'

Llewellyn raised dark eyebrows that were as neat as the
rest of him and said, 'Something along the lines of "We're
proceeding with our enquiries and have a number of
promising leads", you mean?'

'That'll do for starters.' He threw a coin across the desk.
'Get me a cup of tea from the canteen, will you? While
you're doing that, you can think up a few more bunches of
bullshit. One of the muggers was thought to be Asian so I'm
sure you can work in something about ethnic sensitivities
while you're at it. A few such lines should keep him off my
back for a while.'

'Wouldn't it be easier to investigate the muggings?'

'Probably. Tell me when you run out of the right lines in

PC-speak and I'll think about it. Oh –' he shouted just before the door closed behind his sergeant – 'get me a hot cross bun while you're at it.'

Llewellyn's head reappeared. 'I think you'll find it should be called a hot *lined* bun now. Religious symbolism is also on the veto list.'

'Veto my arse. Not by me, it's not.' But Llewellyn had gone.

Rafferty sighed. Because no matter how many politically-correctly worded explanations for his lack of progress on the muggings Llewellyn came up with to appease the super, he supposed he'd have to do a little something about the case no matter how limited his taste for it. He pulled a thin file on the investigation towards him and began to read.

He was interrupted by the ringing of the phone. It was the superintendent.

'Ah. Rafferty. You're in, then?'

The intimation that he had been late wasn't lost on Rafferty. 'Here, bright, shining and ready to go.'

'Good. You can start by going along to my office. I want to talk to you about these muggings.'

The superintendent was in lecturing mode. 'You'll have to do better than this you know, Rafferty.' Superintendent Bradley waved a thin sheaf of papers in the air under Rafferty's nose. 'Your reports are sparse, very sparse. You don't seem to have done a lot.'

Rafferty began his explanatory spiel, wishing the super had rung after Llewellyn had come back from the canteen and primed him with the correct verbiage. He did his best. But his best evidently wasn't good enough because the super interrupted him before he'd got out more than a couple of sentences.

'It won't do, Rafferty. It won't do at all. I want you to apply yourself much harder to solving these cases. I've had the deputy chief constable on my back about them. One of the moneylenders involved is a golfing buddy. You know how little I like to get on the wrong side of the brass. If I do, you'll get on the wrong side of me. Do I make myself clear?'

As crystal, thought Rafferty as he nodded and made his

escape. Just his luck that one of the moneylenders whose collector had been mugged had friends in high places. It meant that Bradley would stay tight on his tail till the investigation was solved. It was a bad start to a day that only got worse.

He'd barely got back to his office when the phone went again. It was Abra, full of the wedding – something he'd thought he'd postponed till the evening.

'Hi, Joe. I've been ringing around a few of the venues. I can't get them to drop their prices. I wondered how much to spend.' She named a figure that made Rafferty's eyes water.

'How much?' he said. 'All that for a measly chicken salad? What do they do, rob graves in their spare time?'

'It's a normal quotation, Joe. You're behind the times. What did you have served at your first wedding? Chip butties all round at the corner chippie?'

He didn't dignify that with a reply. 'Look, Abra, can we talk about this tonight? I'm up to my eyes here.'

'You're always up to your eyes, according to you. I'd have thought planning our wedding would be as important to you as solving a few muggings. Muggings are ten a penny but our wedding will only happen once.' Abra's tone was acerbic and it was with some difficulty that he placated her and got off the phone. That was two people he'd upset and it wasn't even ten o'clock yet. When the phone rang for the third time he braced himself. He was right to do so. It was Uniformed reporting a suspected murder.

'Where?'

'In an alleyway adjacent to Primrose Avenue.'

'How was he killed?'

'Several blows to the back of his head.'

'Any idea of the victim's identity?'

'Not immediately, no. His wallet's missing. Though Constable Lizzie Green thinks he's a man called John "Jaws" Harrison. Works as a collector for Malcolm Forbes, one of the local loan sharks.'

Oh great, thought Rafferty. He put the phone down, gulped his now lukewarm tea and bit into his hot cross bun, while he brooded on the investigation and how to keep

Superintendent Bradley off his back. With the latest phone call, Rafferty knew he would have to do rather more than 'a little something' about the loan shark muggings. Especially now they'd escalated to murder.

Two

In spite of the deceptively pretty name of Primrose Avenue, the road beside the alley where the murder had happened was in a run-down area of Elmhurst on the southern outskirts of the town, the houses mostly rented from the council or from buy-to-let private landlords, with unofficial lodgers taken in to help pay the rent. Here lived Elmhurst's low-end population: the single mothers, the unemployed and un-employable, people in their fifties unable to find work, pensioners, the chronically sick and so on.

The dead man had been attacked in the alleyway that ran behind the left-hand-side row of terraced houses. Both the alley and the houses ended in a high brick wall belonging to a canning factory so were effectively culs-de-sac.

Their cadaver had clearly been robbed as there was no wallet or mobile phone on his body, nor any other means of easy identification. He lay partially on his side. His face, from what Rafferty could see of it, bore a surprised look. He had been struck from behind and then his attacker had continued to rain down blows on his head, though fortunately they had mostly been to the back of his skull so they should have less trouble identifying him than might otherwise have been the case.

Rafferty struggled to keep the umbrella aloft in the high wind as it was almost torn from his grasp. He huddled into his thin raincoat and prayed for summer as he stared at the dead man's face. He couldn't help but think that this was somehow Llewellyn's fault. If he hadn't said that today looked likely to be quiet maybe Rafferty wouldn't be standing out in a howling gale doing a poor man's rendition of *Singing in the Rain*. But without the singing. Or the dancing, unless the jig of his umbrella counted. 'You know,' he said to

Llewellyn, a smidgeon of blame in his voice that he knew was unfair, 'Lizzie Green thought the victim was a John Harrison who works for Malcolm Forbes. I think she's right.' It was the confirmation he had feared ever since Uniformed's phone call.

Llewellyn nodded. 'I thought that, too.'

Malcolm 'The Enforcer' Forbes was one of the local loan sharks, who ran his business from the back room of his pawnbroker's shop. 'The victim's nicknamed "Jaws", if I remember rightly. And not only on account of his gnashers.' The large, protruding teeth should have provided him with the dead man's ID immediately. With such a face, he looked particularly suited to the job of loan shark's gofer. His was a familiar face in the neighbourhood. John 'Jaws' Harrison was something of a poacher turned gamekeeper. A man who had got deeply in debt to Malcolm Forbes and who had offered his services to Forbes as a collector in order to pay them off. And as he was built like the proverbial brick outhouse with a face to match, his offer to demand money with menaces had been taken up.

'Should have stayed in debt, mate,' Rafferty advised the corpse. 'You might have stayed alive. There's nothing worse than shitting on your own doorstep for breeding hatreds, especially when you worked for a bloke like Forbes.'

He stood pondering his own profundity for several moments as he stared at the corpse and took in his appearance. Whoever had hit him had done a thorough job. The skull was visibly dented, with crusted blood congealed in the light brown hair. The man was wearing thick black brogues and green corduroy trousers. His raincoat, a pale fawn, was rucked up under the body. It had absorbed water from the muddy puddles decorating the alley. Altogether, he looked a sorry corpse.

Llewellyn, after a brief glance behind him, suggested, 'Perhaps we should let the photographer do his work?'

It seemed like a good idea to Rafferty as he now became aware of what a logjam had built up behind them: Lance Edwards, the photographer; Fraser, the fingerprints king; Adrian Appleby and his Scene of Crime team were all kicking their heels at the alley's entrance, awaiting their turn at the cadaver and its environs. Before they knew it the usually tardy Dr Sam 'Dilly' Dally would arrive and would expect proprietorship of the corpse and all its works.

They made their way back to the alley's entrance and stripped off their protective gear. 'He's all yours,' Rafferty told Lance Edwards as he folded up the umbrella, having given up his losing battle with the wind.

'Want me to get the house-to-house organized?' Llewellyn asked. 'And a thorough search of the alley?'

Rafferty nodded. He glanced up the street to where a gaggle of shaven-headed youths stood on the corner trying to look cool and pretending to be impervious to the chilly weather in their bum-freezer leather jackets and threadbare jeans. Rafferty wasn't interested in being 'cool'. Neither was he ashamed of showing weakness by shivering. It *was* bloody cold, after all. The youths had been there when he and Llewellyn had arrived. Perhaps they'd been there earlier when Jaws Harrison had turned up? If so, they must now be so 'cool' as to be frozen to the marrow, though he supposed the first one to admit it would be chicken. 'Once you've organized a search of the alley you can start the house-to-house with them,' he told Llewellyn. 'And get Uniform to put a crime tape around the end of the alley and street before we have day-trippers gawping at our efforts.'

After Llewellyn had gone off to do his bidding, Rafferty stood, taking in the scene. Now that he'd arrived to put a sting in Uniformed's tail the cordons were going across and the erection of a tent over the corpse had begun. The Scene of Crime team had now started a fingertip search of the alley. Someone had found a hedge-trimmer a few yards up the alley from the body. Briefly, Rafferty wondered what it was doing there and whether it had had anything to do with the murder. Along the short terraced cul-de-sac of fourteen houses, women were standing in little huddles, arms folded against the cold, taking everything in. Doubtless some had already had a good look at the body before the arrival of Uniform. He hoped not too many of them had tramped all over his crime scene and contaminated it.

Rafferty asked PC Timothy Smales, one of the Uniformed officers, who had found the body. Young Smales pointed to the area car where a man could be discerned sitting in the back, before he consulted his notebook. 'Over there, sir. Name of Eric Lewis. Lives at number four. There's a bit of a discrepancy. He says he found the body between three and three thirty, but it wasn't rung in till five o'clock.'

Rafferty was impressed. Young Smales was coming along just fine. One time, he wouldn't have been able to supply such information so readily. 'I'll have a word.' Rafferty, glad of an excuse to get out of the wind and rain, walked over to the car and dropped into the front passenger seat. 'Mr Lewis? I'm DI Rafferty. I understand you found the body?'

Mr Lewis nodded, but added no further explanation. He was a stocky man of around the mid-forties, with heavy jowls and hardly any hair. Though he bore a remarkable look of television's one-time TV cop, Kojak, he didn't have the ever-present lollipop.

'And this was around three to half past?'

This brought another nod.

'I gather from one of my officers that it wasn't rung in till five o'clock. Why the delay?'

Lewis said nothing for several moments, then, 'I was in shock, wasn't I? I wasn't thinking straight. I could barely get my head around it.'

Rafferty, doubting the man had been so shocked that he'd been incapable of picking up a phone, noted his excuse for future probing. 'Was he dead when you found him?'

'I didn't stop to look. But he must have been to judge from the state of the back of his head. Caved in it was.'

Still is, thought Rafferty. Not a pretty sight and him with a canteen meal still sitting heavily. 'Did you recognize him?'

'Who? Me? No. Never saw him before in my life.'

That sounded unlikely to Rafferty, seeing as Mr Lewis lived in the street from where, according to Ma's gossip, Jaws Harrison regularly collected. However, for the moment, he didn't press the point. His ma only lived around the corner and knew all the neighbours' business better than they knew it themselves. He'd have a word with her later and see what she could tell him about their current crop of suspects.

'You live at number four, Mr Lewis, on the opposite side of the street, I understand?' Lewis nodded. 'I wondered what you were doing in that alleyway, seeing as it's a dead end and doesn't lead anywhere apart from the back entrances to the houses on the other side of the avenue.'

'I borrowed a hedge-trimmer from Jim Jenkins at number eleven and was returning it. He's a bit mutt and Jeff and I knew he wouldn't hear me if I knocked at the front. Spends most of his time in the back garden or the back room. He's of the generation that kept the front room for "best"', he added as an afterthought.

'My officers found a hedge-trimmer close to the body. How did it get there?'

'I must have dropped it when I saw the body. Maybe one of your lot will give it back to Jim.'

'All in good time. Did you see anybody about when you found the body?'

'Only a few kids and the yobs on the corner. They're always hanging about and making a nuisance of themselves.' A note of complaint entered Lewis's voice. 'We call your lot regular, but nothing's ever done.'

'I see,' Rafferty said, unwilling to get started on that particular losing argument. He eased his back for a moment from where it was twisted in the passenger seat in order to talk to Eric Lewis. 'And these are the same yobs who were there when I arrived?'

'Yeah. I told you, they're always hanging about. Got nothing better to do than catcall everyone who passes them. The parents do nothing. Glad to get them out of the house probably and have them torment someone else for a change.'

'And you said they generally hang about at the end of the street?'

'Yeah.'

'So they probably saw anyone who entered the alley?'

'I suppose.'

'You don't seem very sure.'

'Told you, I'm in shock. Besides, I don't want it getting back to them that I mentioned them at all. They can be nasty little bastards. Especially that Jake Sterling. He must be known to your lot. He spends his life causing trouble. His brother Jason's no better.'

'I see. You can rest assured they won't hear anything about our conversation from me.'

'Don't need to, do they? They've all got eyes in their spiky heads. I saw them give me a few throat-slashing gestures when I got in the car. You were talking to that other copper at the time. Don't suppose you noticed.'

Eric Lewis's lack of confidence in the police was clearly far-reaching. Still, Rafferty supposed, with yobs like Jake and Jason Sterling to contend with on a daily basis, the man was entitled to feel disgruntled.

'Why would they threaten you? Do you think one or more of them might have something to do with this man's death?'

'Don't know.' He paused, then added, 'I told you I didn't know the dead bloke. How am I supposed to know if they had reason to bear him a grudge?'

Rafferty, by now tired of skirting around the subject, attacked it head on. 'We know the identity of the victim, Mr Lewis. I'm surprised you don't, seeing as he collected money from this street regularly.' Rafferty could only hope his ma's gossip was accurate. But the thought that it was invariably spot on encouraged him. 'Several of the street residents must have had reason to loathe the man. He wasn't known as "Jaws" solely because of his appearance. It's my under-standing that his disposition wasn't of the nicest to those unable to make their loan instalments. Perhaps you were one of them?'

'No. Certainly not. I–I don't get things on credit. If I can't pay for something I do without.'

'Very commendable.' Though it was a novel sentiment in these days that were as loose on financial morality as they were on any other sort. Rafferty wished he could say the same. The wedding quotes were still bugging him, of course. They'd end up thousands of pounds in debt if he didn't take things in hand. But he did his best to forget his large, looming debts as he continued his interview. 'We'll have an officer checking with Jaws Harrison's boss to get a list of those in the street who owed him money and were having difficulty repaying their loans. But you've said you won't be on the list of debtors, so . . .'

Mr Lewis spluttered incoherently for a few seconds, his

spluttering interspersed with the noise of rain lashing the car windows. He rubbed his bald head, then he blurted out, 'All right. I admit it. I did take a loan out with Forbes. Only a small one, mind. Five hundred quid and I've nearly finished paying it off. But then so did other people in the street and most of them were in hock for much more than me, so don't go pointing the finger in my direction when you look for your killer. It'll be pointed in the wrong place.'

'Oh? And what direction should it be pointed?'

But Lewis wasn't to be drawn. He clammed up at the question. All he said was, 'I wouldn't know, would I? All I know is that it wasn't me who killed him.'

'OK, Mr Lewis, That'll be all for now. But stay in the car. We'll need a formal statement. I'll get one of my officers to drive you to the police station so you can give it.'

Eric Lewis looked alarmed at this. 'Why do I have to go to the police station to give a statement? I've just told you what happened, haven't I? All I did was find the body. I can't say any more than that. I can't see the point in a lot of rigmarole over that.'

Put like that, it *did* seem much ado about nothing. But, as he told Mr Lewis, they had procedures that had to be followed. 'It won't take long. One of my officers will drive you back home.'

Eric Lewis seemed to think it was an invitation that was open to refusal because he continued to prevaricate. 'Well, I don't know. The wife won't like it. Wanted me to start the decorating today.'

Seeing as the day had been far advanced by the time Mr Lewis found the body, he hadn't made a cracking beginning on the painting he was now so keen on. 'Never mind,' Rafferty said. 'You can get an early start in the morning, can't you?'

'Suppose so. Though she still won't like it.'

Rafferty looked out of the rain-lashed windscreen, steeled himself, and got out of the car, leaving Eric Lewis still searching for excuses. It was still pouring. He hunched his shoulders and gestured to one of the Uniforms and told him to drive Lewis to the station and find someone to take his statement. He trudged back towards the alley, fighting the strengthening wind all the way and trying and failing to avoid the large puddles that had grown larger while he had been speaking to Eric Lewis and which made the ends of his trousers uncomfortably soggy. He met Llewellyn coming the other way; Llewellyn, of course, had the wind behind him. To Rafferty's irritation, Llewellyn's umbrella was still holding its own against the elements that had turned his inside out. His trousers were also, somehow, free of puddle damage. 'Got anything?' he asked as he swallowed his irritation at his sergeant's ability to stay looking smart whatever the weather or other people threw at him.

'The youths claim they saw nothing. What about you? How have you got on?'

Rafferty pushed a hand through his dripping hair and scowled. 'I've got precious little. Though Mr Lewis, the man who I was just talking to and who admits to finding the body and ringing it in, did tell me those lads were hanging about when he found the body. You got their details?'

Llewellyn bridled slightly at this. 'Of course.' He patted his pocket. 'I also checked their claimed identities with a couple of the neighbours. Three of the youths supplied false names for reasons they preferred not to go into when I challenged them.'

'Force of habit, probably. So which of them tried to be clever dicks?'

'Jake Sterling, Des Arnott and Tony Moran.'

'They the cocky looking trio in the leather jackets?'

'The very same.'

'OK. What say we haul them all in for questioning? Maybe their little friend lacking the cool leather will be more chatty without the cocksure threesome earwigging his every word.'

'On what charge?'

Rafferty sighed. This was Llewellyn at his most pedantic. 'Try a touch of lateral thinking, Dafyd.' Then, with the recollection that the logical Llewellyn was still having trouble thinking in his own haphazard manner, he said, 'Obstructing the police sounds favourite to me. Maybe also threatening behaviour seeing as Mr Lewis said they made throat-slitting gestures at him. Should be worth a few hours of their time. How's the house-to-house going?'

'Most of the street residents have given preliminary

statements, though not everyone was at home so they'll have to be followed up later. They're still searching the alley. We're also questioning the residents of the houses that form a T-junction with Primrose Avenue. They might have seen something.'

'Anyone admitted to seeing anything? Anything at all?'

Llewellyn shook his head. 'Though, as I said, we have yet to question everyone.' His hair was still dry, its style still immaculate, which made Rafferty feel even more irritated. After all, it had been Llewellyn who had tempted the fates.

Rafferty, already in an ill humour and determined to think the worst, ignored Llewellyn's last comment. 'So we've got the proverbial see no evil and hear no evil. Great. I suppose it's inevitable given the identity of the victim. All the people who owed money to Jaws Harrison's boss will be glad to see the end of him and his heavy-handed tactics.'

'Most of the residents wouldn't even admit to knowing Mr Harrison,' Llewellyn said, raising his soft voice against the howling wind. 'Stupid, really, as we shall shortly have records of the debtors in the street from Mr Forbes.'

'Mmm. Instinctive reaction I suppose. Speak first, in denial, and think about what you've said afterwards. No one wants to be connected to murder. Have you sent someone to get the debtor list from his office?'

'I was just about to.'

'Send Lizzie Green. Maybe her particular feminine touch will ease things along. Got a nice way with her has Lizzie.' Plump in all the right places, Lizzie Green exuded the great-aunt's perfume of lily of the valley talcum power partnered by a Bardotesque pout. It was a curiously erotic combination that warmed Rafferty briefly, even in the face of the stinging rain.

'Anything else?'

'Yeah. Get Lizzie to find out the victim's address and his next of kin while she's at Forbes's office. We'll need to go along once we're finished here and break the news. Oh, and give Dally a bell. See what's keeping him. I'm keen to learn as quickly as possible if our victim died in that alley seeing as how it should lessen the number of potential suspects.'

Llewellyn walked off clutching his mobile and his

umbrella, still looking as pristine as at his arrival, while Rafferty, by now so wet through that he felt he could get no wetter, resigned, planted his feet firmly as anchorage against the wind and did some more studying of the location. The cul-de-sac was made up of fourteen terraced houses, seven on each side of the road with parking on the street. Each house had a tiny front garden separating it from the road. Two or three were well kept, with pots of now battered and mostly petal-less spring bulbs brightening them, but most housed rusty bikes and weeds. The houses on the left backed on to the alley where the dead man had been found. *Had* he died there? Rafferty wondered again. Or had he been taken there after being killed elsewhere? And how come no one saw anything? It was broad daylight and although the street, owing to its dead-end nature, would have lacked casual visitors, there were still kids about, it being the Easter holidays, and women going to and from the local parade of shops. And what of the youths who claimed to have seen nothing? True, the dead man had been found between numbers eleven and thirteen – unlucky for some – around the bend in the alley and out of their line of vision, but they must have seen him enter the alley and know roughly what time he had arrived in the street. Was this killing merely an escalation in the violence of the previous muggings or was it something more? A planned and deliberately executed killing? Could it be that a turf war had broken out among the local loan sharks? But if that was the case, Rafferty argued to himself, surely the murder would have been much more showy and designed to serve as a warning. Whoever did it, given the number and ferocity of the blows, had certainly been determined to remove Jaws Harrison from this world.

Three

Rafferty caught up with two of the Uniformed officers on house-to-house duties. 'I'll want a list of everyone in the street ASAP. Especially those in the odd house numbers one to thirteen. They had the best access to the alley. How many people are we talking about on that side of the street?'

'Adults and mid-teens, it's thirteen, sir,' replied Constable Claire Allen, the newest member of the team, after she had done a swift tally up.

There was that number again, thought Rafferty, his superstitious side giving him goose-bumps. He hoped it wasn't going to turn out to be as unlucky for him as it had been for Jaws Harrison.

'How many of the thirteen look possibles?'

'Ten, sir. One of the thirteen is a woman in an advanced stage of pregnancy and two are elderly and look rather frail.'

'Appearances can be deceptive. If you're desperate enough you'll find reserves of strength from somewhere. I reckon some of these people must have been beyond desperate if they owed Malcolm Forbes money they were unable to pay and with the dead man making threats.'

Rafferty sent the pair on their way as he spotted Sam Dally's car draw up beyond the cordon. He hurried to speak to him. According to Dally, when he'd cursed at the weather, the rain making his sparse hair look even thinner, and had finally wriggled his rotund body into his protective gear and checked out the body, the hypostasis evidence pointed to the man having died where he was found.

'Right-handed assailant, as the majority of the blows are to the right-hand side of the skull. I'm not sure of the weapon used; round-ended, like a hammer, but I don't think it was a hammer – or not one that I've ever seen. Certainly something with metal rather than wood at the end as I can't see any splinters in the wounds, though I will, of course, do a thorough check during the post-mortem. I suppose you also want a time of death?'

'If you can.' It was now five thirty.

'Certainly within the last three, three and a half hours, erring more towards two to two and a half I would think. Will that do you?'

'It'll do me very nicely, Sam. Much obliged.'

'That's what I'm here for.' His rain-spattered half-moon glasses glinted as the sun came out for a few seconds, saw the weather and went back to bed. 'And don't order your underlings to chase me up in future. You know how I hate to be rushed.'

Rafferty nodded. 'Sorry and all that.' Dally by name and dally by nature, that was Sam. Not that he didn't do a thorough job, which was why Rafferty put up with the Scotsman's irascibility.

'Got an ID yet?'

'We believe so. A collector for a local loan shark named Malcolm Forbes. So we've got a motive likely to apply to a number of our suspects.'

'Och. There'll not be too many loose tongues, then. Not talking to the police, anyway. Though they'll doubtless be happy to curry favour with your man Forbes if they know anything. Likely there'll be some willing to tell porkies to get in well with him. Could be an opportunity for one or two to settle old scores.'

'That's what I'm afraid of. An early post-mortem would be good, Sam.'

'Would it, now? Always in a rush, Rafferty, that's your trouble. You've got enough to be going on with, I'd say. Leave the timing of the post-mortem to them as knows what else is awaiting attention. I'll get back to you.' With that, Dally picked up his bag of tricks and fought his rotund way back down the alley.

Now he had a likely weapon, Rafferty set some of the team to checking the sheds and outhouses for missing hammers and other metal-headed tools. The search of the alley had turned up nothing but the usual rubbish of discarded cigarette and crisp packets.

After having a quick word with Adrian Appleby, head of the SOCO team, Rafferty, relieved to get out of the reach of the weather again, picked up a loitering Llewellyn and drove back to the station. On the way, they discussed the case.

'I'm worried this might be something more than a routine mugging gone wrong,' Rafferty confided as he overtook a slow-moving milk cart. He noticed Llewellyn – always a nervous passenger when Rafferty was behind the wheel – clutch the edge of his seat with white-knuckled hands as the speedometer touched fifty-five. He eased back on the accelerator as he passed the milk float and said, 'You can let the seat go now. I was only doing fifty.'

'In a thirty-mile limit,' Llewellyn pointed out. 'That's breaking the law. And the wet roads won't help with braking distances.'

Rafferty's lips pursed at this, but he said nothing further about it. 'As I said, this case has all the hallmarks of a turf war.'

'Possibly,' said Llewellyn, dampeningly. 'But we ought to wait until we've got more evidence before we come to any conclusions.'

'I haven't come to any conclusions. I'm just wondering, that's all.'

Nothing further was said, but there was the beginning of a strained atmosphere by the time their journey ended.

On their arrival back at the station and before he did anything else, Rafferty popped into the gents'. His hair was dripping annoyingly down the back of his neck and his wet trouser ends flapped around his ankles with each step. He got the worst of the wet off each under the hand dryer, propped up on one of the sinks to do his trousers. Back at his desk, it wasn't long before he was in possession of the list he had requested of adults and juveniles living in the houses on the oddly-numbered side of the street. As Claire Allen had said, there were thirteen all told, including the pregnant single mother Tracey Stubbs, who lived at number nine and the two pensioners, Mrs Emily Parker and Mr Jim Jenkins, both of whom lived alone and whose houses were numbered thirteen and eleven respectively.

Of the thirteen, Billy Jones, the younger son of the Joneses at number five, claimed to have been at work at the canning factory that backed on to both Primrose Avenue and the alley; another, Dennis Jones, the elder son, claimed to have been at the Job Centre on Elmhurst's High Street from two fifteen to three thirty; and a third, Anthony Clifford of number three, said he had been putting up shelves at his soon-to-be mother-in-law's two streets away prior to when the body was found. That still left ten of the residents who had the greatest opportunity to murder Harrison. Some of the other residents were with family members the whole time, so unless there had been collusion between them, their potential as suspects was lessened though not completely out of the park. A lot depended on what they managed to get out of the youths. If Sam Dally's time of death was as accurate as it usually was, most would be in the clear. Providing, that was, their stories checked out. That left a bunch of students at number seven who all seemed to be out, Mr and Mrs Jones who were both unemployed and lived at number five along with their two sons and the lodger Peter Allbright, Anthony Clifford's live-in partner Josie McBride at number three, Samantha Dicker, the lodger at number one, the pregnant Tracey Stubbs, plus the two pensioners. The family at number one, it had finally been ascertained, were currently on holiday in Spain, though their lodger, Samantha Dicker, said she had been in the property at the estimated time of Harrison's murder.

The residents on the other side of the street whose back gardens adjoined a separate alley were also questioned, but as they didn't have immediate, discreet access to the murder scene, as suspects they featured lower down the list.

Of immediate interest was who might have had a motive for murder. He rang Lizzie Green on her mobile. 'Lizzie, how are you doing on getting that list of Forbes's debtors in Primrose Avenue?'

'I've got it, sir, as well as the details of the dead man's next of kin. He was living with a woman called Annie Pulman in a flat off the High Street.' She rattled off the address. 'I'm on my way back to the nick.'

'Good man. Come straight to my office. If we can do some mixing and matching on opportunity and motive, we might get somewhere sooner than expected.'

'Yes sir. I'll see you soon.'

Rafferty replaced the receiver and sat back, contemplating the ceiling. He'd given up smoking, but would give anything for a drag or two right now. But he refused to give in to the craving. Instead, he would have to rely on that other stalwart crutch for cases of emergency. He needed tea, hot and sweet. It helped him to think. Or so he believed. It would, anyway, help him get through the next few hours. He walked to the office door and opened it, collaring Timothy Smales who was passing by. 'Finished with Eric Lewis and his statement?'

'Yes sir.' He handed the paperwork over.

'Get me and Sergeant Llewellyn some tea, son, and take your break when you've got it.' Mission accomplished, Rafferty returned to his chair. The ceiling having proved unhelpful as a provider of answers, he contemplated his navel instead. But all it told him was that he was getting the beginnings of a paunch. He was glad when Lizzie knocked on the door and brought in the list of Primrose Avenue debtors.

Six of those in the odd side of the street who were at home and had the opportunity to kill also had large debts with Malcolm Forbes. The rest, on the surface at least, had no motive that they had yet discerned. But it was early days. Too soon to be leaping to conclusions as Llewellyn would undoubtedly tell him if he was foolish enough to voice an opinion so early in the investigation. Still, he reasoned, those six were the most interesting to a suspicious policeman. He'd question them and see what they had to say for themselves. But he'd wait until after the PM. He wanted to have a more certain idea of the time of death than he currently had before he questioned anyone further, apart from the four street-corner-hanging youths.

As soon as he'd had a good idea from Sam Dally of what had been the most likely murder weapon, he'd set a couple of the Uniforms on checking out back gates and shed doors for locks. None of the back gates had either locks or bolts and few of the sheds. Anyone with a mind to could have

entered the back garden of one of the houses, helped themselves to a hammer or some other tool, and waited for Jaws
to come along. On the surface, those with gardens that backed
on to the alley where it curved would have had the best
chance of killing him out of sight of the youths at the top
of the alley. But the youths would doubtless have spent their
time moving and mucking about so wouldn't necessarily
have a view down the alley all the time so he couldn't remove
the residents of the lower house numbers from his suspect
list. Any of the residents of the entire row could have waited
their chance, nipped along the alley while the youths amused
themselves further up the street and then slipped around the
curve in the alley and into a neighbour's back garden while
they waited for the collector.

So far, they had eight possible suspects; even the very
pregnant Tracey Stubbs could have wielded a hammer from
behind the victim without too much strain. So could everyone
else. That was the problem. But at least the five students in
number seven had, it had been discovered, all gone back to
their family homes for the holidays. They had been checked
out and exonerated.

They'd started a check for the weapon and had asked the
four corner-loitering youths who amongst the residents had
left the street and who might have disposed of the same after
the time Dr Dally said the murder had been committed. After
a brief show of bravado, Tony Moran, one of the less cocky
youths, had provided some answers. He had admitted to
hanging around the street corner for most of the afternoon,
mucking about and being rude to passers-by.

'It was only a bit of fun, like,' he artlessly confided.

'I presume you saw the victim, Mr Harrison, enter the
alley?'

Moran nodded.

'And did you see anyone leave Primrose Avenue after
you'd seen Mr Harrison?'

'Yeah. I saw a few women going to the shops. Two – no,
three.'

'And do you know their names?' Llewellyn asked.

Moran shook his head. 'I'm no good with names.'

'Can you describe them?'

'Yeah, I suppose.' He proceeded to do so and Llewellyn nodded to confirm he recognized the women concerned.

'So,' said Rafferty as they left Tony Moran to be escorted back to his cell and Llewellyn had confided the identities of the women Moran had described, 'if we fail to find the weapon, the three women who left the street for a short time – Mrs Jones, Mrs Parker and Josie McBride – were the only ones who could have disposed of it away from Primrose Avenue.

'Check whether we've got any previous for any of the residents, Dafyd, plus the two youths who don't live on the street: Des Arnott and Tony Moran. You'll probably find a few drunk-and-disorderlies and affrays as well, but I'm looking for something more meaty. It might give us a lead.'

They entered the office and Llewellyn turned to his computer. Rafferty addressed himself to his tea, which Timothy Smales had just delivered. Shortly after he had the answers: Jake, the elder of the two Sterling boys, was, it seemed, well in the frame for a mugging gone wrong as he'd had a chequered criminal career for one so young.

'Apart from Jake Sterling and his friend, Des Arnott, no one has been up on any serious charges. A certain amount of brawling is the worst,' Llewellyn said.

'And that's just the women,' Rafferty joked. 'A one-off killer then. It always pointed that way. Oh well, now you've dashed my hopes, can you attempt to replace them with better ones?'

'I can but try.' Llewellyn studied him for a moment with his serious brown eyes. 'The psychological angle—' he began.

'No.' Rafferty groaned. 'No. Please. Not that. No mumbo-jumbo. If this isn't the first shot in a turf war, this is your typical act of madness with a certain amount of premedita-tion thrown in, to my way of thinking. The weapon at the ready suggests that.'

'Not necessarily,' Llewellyn objected. 'The murderer, like Mr Jones at number five, could simply have been innocently doing a few odd jobs in the garden when he or she saw their chance.'

'And grabbed it. Mmm. I suppose you're right.' Frustratingly, Llewellyn usually was. 'OK. Scrub that theory. Any other ideas?'

'To return to the psychological angle—'

'Let's not. I told you, it's something meaty I want. How many hammers are we missing?'

'Three. One each from the sheds of numbers one, three and eleven. But as those sheds were as lacking in locks as the back gates it gets us no further forward. Anyone could have helped themselves from most of the garden sheds along the row.'

'You're no use, are you? I ask you to give me hope and all you do is give me facts I already know.' Rafferty slumped back in his chair and returned to his study of the ceiling. 'Throw me a few straws I can clutch at, for God's sake.'

'I'm not a great believer in straw-clutching.'

'No, you're not, are you? Perhaps I should try young Timmy Smales. I might at least find a straw behind his wet ear.' Though even that hope evaporated as he recalled that Smales's ears were beginning to dry up nicely. Which was more than his were doing as he felt like he had half the Atlantic lodged there. He found a grubby tissue in his drawer and dried them.

The murder had occurred in a part of town which frequently required the presence of Uniform: domestics, neighbourly disputes and troublesome youths causing a nuisance. Ma's house, only a few streets away, was different again. Most of the occupants of her road were older and had bought their houses from the council. They had a pride in keeping them spruce. The name Primrose Avenue conjured up an aura of faded gentility that was at odds with reality. The terraced housing had been built after the war and the land had originally been fields adjoining a stream which had been drained at the time the houses went up. There were few primroses to be seen there now.

He turned back to Llewellyn who, with Rafferty's intent study of the ceiling, had returned back to the batch of early statements at his corner desk. 'None of Malcolm Forbes's debtors mentioned Jaws Harrison knocking on their doors?'

Llewellyn shook his head. 'Not according to house-to-house.' Llewellyn's brown eyes were thoughtful. 'I'd like to know what he was doing in that alleyway where he died.'

Rafferty smiled. That one was easy, as he told his sergeant.

'I imagine he was in that alleyway because he knew he wouldn't get an answer if he knocked on the front door. Probably, he had nous enough to know that debtor families with kids leave the back door unlocked. Probably, he didn't keep to a strict routine on his collection round, either. If he had any sense, he would have liked the element of surprise. He was also probably scared of getting mugged given the two cases last week. He'd usually have a tidy sum, I imagine, by the time he'd finished his collections.'

'So nobody could have known precisely when he'd turn up?'

'That's what I'm thinking. But you can check it out. If I'm right, it must have made it more difficult to plan his murder – if planning was actually involved and it wasn't just an opportunistic assault.'

'Clearly not *too* difficult, considering he's dead.'

'True.' Rafferty sighed and put his feet up on his desk. His shoes were dulled from their contact with the deep puddles in Primrose Avenue. He'd have felt aggrieved at that if they hadn't been pretty dull to begin with. No Beau Brummel, him. 'Perhaps the adults used the kids as lookouts and got warning of his arrival?' The children on the street were currently on their Easter holidays from school, and even though the weather had been cold and wet most of them would have been playing out on their own and neighbouring streets and easily able to warn mum and dad of Jaws's arrival.

The victim had been killed in broad daylight yet no one had seen a thing. Or so they claimed. Had his killer really not appreciated that his tormentor would be quickly replaced? Or had fear and desperation simply clouded their judgement? Was any break from the debt collection, however brief, a welcome respite? Overcome by misery, despair and hatred of their persecutor, had they just struck out at the local face of their tormentor when the opportunity presented itself, so that, for once, someone else was the victim?

It seemed plausible. Desperation could drive people to commit all sorts of illogical acts. It would have made more sense if they'd targeted the boss man himself, Malcolm Forbes. A petrol bomb lobbed through his letterbox in the middle of the night, home and office both, would have removed him and the debtors' records.

Instead, the killer – whom Rafferty presumed must be numbered amongst those who owed Forbes money – had chosen to remove one of Forbes's collectors. Pointless really.

Four

'It's time we got over to Jaws Harrison's home and broke the news of his death,' Rafferty said as he finished his tea, shortly after. 'You stay here and carry on reading those statements,' he told Llewellyn. 'I'll take Lizzie Green with me.'

John Jaws Harrison lived in a small first-floor flat off the High Street. A slatternly-looking blonde answered the door.

'Yeah? What do you want?' she asked after they had shown her their IDs. Her expression was sullen and unwelcoming. It seemed police officers were not her favourite people. Rafferty hurried to explain the reason for their visit.

'If we could come in for a few minutes? I'm afraid we have some bad news for you.'

'Bad news? What bad news?' She stood, arms folded, barring their way, her expression suspicious as if she thought they were trying to gain entry under false pretences.

Rafferty tried again. 'It's about Mr Harrison,' he began. 'He—'

'What's happened to him? Tell me.' Her thin, bony hands were clenched into fists as if she was considering striking them.

Gently, Rafferty took her arm and persuaded her up the stairs and down the narrow hall to the living room. Once he'd got her seated, he broke the news.

'Dead? He can't be dead. I only saw him this morning.'

'I'm afraid it's true, Ms Pulman.'

She took a few moments to absorb this, then she asked, 'So how did he die? Did he have an accident in his car?'

'No. It was nothing like that. I'm afraid we have reason to believe he was murdered.'

Her eyes, with their thick surround of eyeliner and lashings of mascara, rounded at this. Then she began to sob loudly.

'I'll make some tea,' Lizzie volunteered, to Rafferty's dismay, leaving him with the sobbing woman. He patted Annie Pulman's stiff back with a tentative hand. But the tea was quickly made and Lizzie was soon back.

'Did Mr Harrison have any enemies that you know of?' he asked Annie Pulman's bowed head. It shook in response. Her eye make-up had begun to smear and run, making black tracks with her tears through the thick foundation on her face. Rafferty looked around for a box of tissues, and seeing none, he went in search of the bathroom and came back trailing a length of toilet paper. Silently, he handed it to her.

Clearly she was in denial, given Harrison's job was designed to make enemies. 'Have you lived together long?'

'Six months,' she spluttered between gulping sobs.

She could tell them little; she knew nothing about Harrison's job beyond that he was a debt collector.

'Did he have any family? Parents? Brothers or sisters?'

'No, his parents are dead. He had one brother, but he emigrated to Australia ten years ago. I don't know where he lives. John hasn't heard from him in ages.'

It didn't leave much choice about who would have to do the formal identifying. Tentatively, he mentioned this to Annie Pulman, but all he received in return was a shocked stare. 'Maybe later,' he murmured soothingly.

After another five minutes of this, Rafferty said, 'I'll leave Constable Green with you. Let her know if there's anyone she can call to be with you.'

He received no acknowledgement to this. But as there was nothing else he could do here for the moment, he left them, confident that Lizzie would cope. He needed to get back to the station.

Jake Sterling and Des Arnott, the cockiest of the leather-clad youths who had been hanging around on the corner of Primrose Avenue with Jake's brother and another mate, were just as cocky an hour later as, one after the other, they sat in interview room two. Rafferty had seen numerous youths like this pair pass through the police station – the country had an entire generation of them; those who knew all about their 'rights', but nothing at all about their responsibilities.

They had been interviewed separately. So far, all they had contributed were sneering 'no comment's to Rafferty and Llewellyn's questions. Rafferty blamed the police programmes on the telly, which were full of youths like these two with their own 'no comment's.

'You know I could charge you with wasting police time?' he told Jake Sterling.

Sterling gave a careless shrug of his head with its grade one haircut. The gesture said it was all the same to him.

It probably was, too. Jake Sterling and Des Arnott knew the score. They'd been here before, both of them. So had Jake's brother, Jason, though Tony Moran, the youngest of the quartet, so far had a clean score sheet.

The duty solicitor – Jake, knowing his rights, had demanded a brief from the off – looked as bored with the proceedings as Jake Sterling himself. He gazed into space, his pen poised to jot down anything of interest that Sterling chose to say. So far, his lined pad was as pristine as a fluffy summer cloud.

'You don't deny giving me a false name?' Llewellyn asked.

Sterling gave another shrug.

'Was that a "yes" shrug or a "no" shrug?' Rafferty asked, beginning to lose his temper. He'd had his fill of surly youths like Sterling. His brother Jason was coming along nicely in the same mould. Doubtless in a few months, Jason too would have the business of frustrating the police down to a fine art.

'One of your friends told us that three women left Primrose Avenue after Jaws Harrison entered the alley. Can you confirm that?' Rafferty asked.

'Yeah, I suppose. Two old biddies and the juicy Josie. I wouldn't mind a go at her.'

'Never mind that. Did you see anyone else leave the avenue?'

'No. Not that I recall. But then I can't say I'm interested in the doings of a bunch of old fogies. Boring farts. All they do is complain and have a go.'

'Perhaps they find the behaviour of you and your friends offensive?' Llewellyn suggested.

Jake Sterling shrugged. 'Whatever.'

This was a waste of time, Rafferty acknowledged to himself. He told the youth and the tapes that the interview was suspended and added the time.

'I can go, right?' Jake demanded.

'So you can say something other than "no comment", then?'

Jake blanked him.

Rafferty got the only satisfaction of the day when he told Sterling, 'No. You can't go. Wasting police time is a serious business, particularly when it involves a murder investigation. We'll probably want another word with you later, so I think we'll hang on to you for now.'

Jake scowled, but as though becoming aware that such a facial contortion didn't gel with the air of cool nonchalance he favoured, he slumped back with an expression that said it was all the same to him.

With Sterling packed off back to his cell, Rafferty suggested they try Tony Moran again. Moran, at eighteen, was the youngest of the four youths brought in for questioning. Like Des Arnott, he didn't live in Primrose Avenue. He lived with his mother in the next street. Surprisingly, given that he hung around with the yobbish Sterlings and Des Arnott, Tony Moran had never been in trouble before. He hadn't even demanded the services of the duty solicitor. Fortunately, Llewellyn had had the wit to ensure the four youths were immediately separated so Moran hadn't had the benefit of Jake's street wisdom. It was fortunate, too, that Moran was over eighteen – just – so they hadn't had to put up with one or both of his parents putting their oar in. Not that it was likely to make any difference. It wasn't as if the Crown Prosecution Service was likely to be interested in proceeding with the cases against them. The most they were likely to get was a caution. Might as well give them a lollipop each for all the notice they'd take of that, to judge from their previous number of visits to the cells. Rafferty's lips tightened, then he asked for Moran to be brought to the interview room.

'So tell me, Tony,' said Rafferty when they had the last of the four youths settled for the second time across the table in the interview room. 'Why did you give a false name to my colleague?'

Moran's lips quivered. 'I dunno. I just copied Jake.'

Rafferty nodded understandingly. 'It seemed like a good idea at the time, hmm?'

Moran nodded. There was an innocence about Tony Moran that his three friends didn't share. The youth seemed to have little guile to him and none of the aggressive confidence that the others exuded with every breath. He appeared nervous and ill-at-ease, his lower lip trembling noticeably.

'Jake Sterling's the leader of your little gang, I take it?'

Moran nodded again.

'For the tape, please.'

'Yeah.'

'So how long have you been a member?'

'Not long. A couple of months.'

'You know they'll get you into serious trouble before long, don't you?'

Moran's expression fought between mutiny and tears. So far it was a draw. 'They're my mates.'

'One for all and all for one?'

Moran frowned at this rare example of Rafferty's limited literary references but nodded. 'Yeah. That's right.'

Poor innocent, thought Rafferty. They'd drop him in it when it suited them. The naïve Moran would be a perfect patsy to the others. It was probably why they'd let him join their gang.

'OK. Now we've got that sorted out. Tell me, Tony, have you remembered anyone else you saw leaving the street, other than the three women you've already told us about?'

'I dunno.'

'Think about it. For instance, did you see Mr Eric Lewis enter the alley with a hedge-trimmer?'

'I saw some old bloke. I don't know his name. He had some gadget or other with him.'

'And what time was this?'

'I dunno. I don't wear a watch.'

Time, mused Rafferty. Keeping track of it was such an inessential to so many modern youths. He often wished it wasn't such an imperative in his own life. 'Just roughly.'

Moran's forehead puckered in thought. 'It must have been some time around three-ish, I suppose, or a bit later. Perhaps it was half past.'

'Do you recall seeing anyone else?'

Moran's forehead did some more puckering. Rafferty, while he was waiting, amused himself by changing one of the vowels in the youth's name on his notepad till he had a surname that was singularly appropriate. *Unkind, Rafferty*, smote his strict Catholic conscience. But it was clear that deep, or even not so deep thought wasn't one of Tony Moran's strong suits.

'I dunno,' he eventually volunteered.

Rafferty swallowed a sigh.

'There were some kids out when I arrived. Playing like.'

Somehow, Rafferty doubted young kids were responsible for Jaws Harrison's murder. But such were the times they lived in, he couldn't totally discount the possibility. 'Do you know their names?'

Perhaps feeling his previous responses had lacked variety, this time Moran just shook his head.

To Rafferty's surprise, Tony Moran then volunteered something. 'Now that I think about it, I remember seeing another bloke on the street this afternoon. I know the faces of everyone in the street.' He should, thought Rafferty, when he spent most of his time hanging around its corner watching his bolder mates causing trouble. 'But this man was a stranger. I'd never seen him before. He carried a briefcase and knocked at number nine.'

Number nine was Tracey Stubbs's home. 'Was he let in?'

Moran nodded. 'Eventually. He was there quite a while.' He grinned. 'According to the lads, that Tracey's a bit of a goer. I wondered if they might be having it off.'

No one else had mentioned seeing this man. Strange that it should be 'I dunno' Moran who supplied the information.

'What did he look like?' Rafferty asked, expecting another 'I dunno'. But Moran surprised him again.

'My mum would call him very smart. Suited and booted. But he was actually a bit flash. I noticed the wind didn't ruffle his hair. It stayed put as if it had been glued to his head. And his suit had a peacock blue lining. I saw it when the wind blew his jacket open. Flash git, I thought.'

A brief memory stirred in Rafferty's head, but was as swiftly gone. 'Anything else you recall about this man?'

Tony Moran's mother seemed to be something of a walking reference book for her son because he again called on her opinion. 'I suppose my mum would have called him a looker. He certainly seemed to fancy himself as he fairly strutted up the street like a cock of the walk. Reckon Tracey must have fancied him as well as he was in her place for ages.'

By dint of tortuous questioning, between them, he and Llewellyn had extracted several pieces of information. Rafferty was as interested in the identities of those who had left the street as in those who had remained, which information Moran had supplied when they had first questioned him. The team had yet to find the murder weapon, so, unless it turned up during the remaining hours of searching, someone had disposed of it. And although Moran was shaky on names and times, he had been able to give them rough descriptions of the women – all of those who had left the street that afternoon had been women – so they had made more progress than Rafferty had expected to at the start of the day.

Rafferty, reluctant to let such a cooperative witness go before they had squeezed him dry of information, glanced at Llewellyn with raised eyebrows. Any more questions? the gesture asked.

Llewellyn nodded. 'Did either you or the other members of your gang enter the alley, before or after the body was found?'

'No.' Moran's answer this time was sharper.

'Did you hear anything? Any cries or arguments, for instance?'

'No. I heard nothing. We were larking about, like. I didn't see or hear nothin'. Neither did the others. They'd have said, like.'

As to whether any of the gang of four had entered the alley, either to follow Harrison with robbery in mind or later, on hearing him cry out, neither Moran nor any of the other three would be likely to admit it. Even Moran wasn't so stupid as to say so if one of them had. Though, unless Jaws's killer had taken the wallet, it seemed the likeliest scenario.

Unless Eric Lewis, seeing the dead body, had decided to help himself, concluding that Forbes's collector would have no more use for it or its contents.

It didn't seem they would get anything further from their witness. According to him, no one other than the victim and Eric Lewis had entered the alley. Lewis had gone in some five or ten minutes after Jaws Harrison, so although well placed to commit murder, he hadn't left the street with the purpose of getting rid of the weapon.

By now, it was eight thirty. In spite of Primrose Avenue, the alley and the surrounding streets and gardens being thoroughly searched, the murder weapon still hadn't turned up. They had found a number of hammers in the sheds and toolboxes of the street, but although they would all be subject to forensic tests, none, so far, showed evidence of having been used in any other way than their manufacturers had intended.

Rafferty suggested they call it a night.

On his way home that evening, Rafferty stopped off at his ma's house. She welcomed him with as much hot sweet tea as he could drink. Settled comfortably in her over-furnished living room, he made swift inroads into the ham sandwiches she also provided. Ma loved to feed people. Now she lived alone she had only herself to cater for, her other five children, like Rafferty himself, were all in relationships and had homes of their own.

Ma settled her rounded body back in her own well-worn, tweed-effect armchair and, the requirements of hospitality over, she said, 'I heard you've got a murder a couple of streets away. The whole neighbourhood's agog.'

'Thought it might be.' Rafferty paused, then asked, 'So who's the favourite for the murder suspect?' He didn't usually go by local gossip in murder investigations, but sometimes the view on the street could be helpful, and at least he'd get the low-down on most of the residents of Primrose Avenue.

'Jake and Jason Sterling seem top of the list. Closely followed by their father, though I'd have thought him too idle to bestir himself to commit murder.'

It was an interesting point of view, particularly as the two youths and their friends had been best placed to spot Jaws Harrison's arrival.

'What do you know about the family?'

'Bunch of wasters.' Ma was always forthright in her views. 'The boys haven't had a job since they left school, but they've had plenty of those ASBO things. They've been tagged and been in youth prison – you must know that as it was your lot who arrested them – but nothing makes any difference. Should have had a short, sharp shock from the start when they began to go off the rails. It might have done some good then. It's all too little too late now.'

'What about the rest of the residents? I'm particularly interested in those on the odd-numbered side of the street. I imagine you know most of the women from your visits to the local shops. Let's start with the lodger at number one, Samantha Dicker.'

'She's a student, studying one of those "ologies" that old telly advert used to go on about. A nice girl on the whole. Up to her eyes in debt, of course, like most students nowadays, though the Smiths are good to her. Treat her like one of the family. They're away in Spain at present, though I suppose you know that?'

Rafferty nodded. 'What about Josie McBride at number three? I gather her and Anthony Clifford are getting married?'

'Yes. Saving like mad according to Josie's mother. She wants a big wedding. I hear it's going to cost over seventeen thousand pounds at the last count.' Ma tutted at such extravagance. 'Stupid lot of nonsense. We didn't spend such ridiculous sums in my day. Didn't have the money, of course. Not that we'd have been so daft as to waste such sums on just one day even if we did have it. It's what comes after that counts. It's my experience that the more money spent on a wedding the shorter the marriage.'

Rafferty nodded. It was his experience, too. Perhaps he could get his ma to put that point of view to Abra?

'Talking of weddings —' his ma began.

'Not now, Ma. Later.' If we must. Get Ma on the subject of weddings, particularly *his*, and they'd be here till midnight with him no further forward in getting a deeper knowledge of his suspects. 'Let's move on to Mr and Mrs Jones at number five and their lodger, Peter Allbright.'

Ma sniffed at being fobbed off her current favourite topic of conversation, but, for once, she obeyed his stricture.

'Harry Jones was made redundant. Must be two years ago now. Hasn't been able to get a job since. Suffers from depression. He's on medication. If it wasn't for the money their youngest boy brings in I don't know how they'd manage.'

'I gather Mrs Jones doesn't work, either?'

'Never has to my knowledge. One of those obsessive housewives and with a husband, the lodger and one of her boys at home all day making a mess, she's got her work cut out. I like a clean house myself, but I don't make myself a martyr to it.'

'But decent people, would you say?'

'They're all right. Not my sort. She always says hello when we meet in the street, though he's got a bit distant lately. It's the depression, I suppose. It's not easy getting another job at his age and it's not as if he's got the skills to go self-employed. No trade, you see. He was only a line worker at one of the factories on the industrial estate.'

'What about the lodger, Peter Allbright?'

'He used to work at the same factory as Harry. That's how he came to lodge with them. Lost his job at the same time as Harry. He's on Jobseeker's Allowance. So was Harry, but I think he's on Incapacity Benefit now.'

'Nice enough bloke, the lodger?'

Ma shrugged. 'Keeps himself to himself. Spends most of his time in his room according to Maggie Jones. No trouble though. He still manages to pay his rent anyway. So that's one blessing. Can't have anything left to live on after that, though. Must be a miserable existence for the lad. He's only around twenty five or so.'

'And Mrs Parker and Mr Jenkins, at numbers thirteen and eleven?' These were the two pensioners. Their frailty alone lessened the likelihood of either being strong suspects. But, as he had told Timothy Smales, appearances could be deceptive, so, as they were both at home at the time of the murder, though only Mrs Parker had a loan with Malcolm Forbes, either had had the opportunity to kill John Jaws Harrison.

'I know Emily Parker from bingo. Nosey sort.' And Ma should know. Like recognizing like and all that. 'I'm surprised she hasn't solved your murder for you. She's always in and out of the neighbours' houses and is the first to know what's going on in the street.' Rafferty had heard this complaint about Emily Parker from his ma before, he recalled. 'Though she wasn't so quick off the mark with this news,' Ma said with satisfaction.

Rafferty smiled to himself. Ma had always seemed of the opinion that knowing everybody's business was *her* job. Clearly, she had a strong challenger in Emily Parker.

'I think the men get fed up with her always in and out. Some of the women, too. And as for Jim Jenkins, he's a bit reserved and not inclined to chat, though I suppose the pain of his arthritis would make anyone miserable. I don't suppose it helps that he lives next door to Tracey Stubbs and her unruly brood. Always kicking footballs into his garden and damaging his vegetables. Rarely stops for a chat, Mr Jenkins. I suppose it makes his legs ache, though he always acknowledges you by doffing his hat. Don't see much of that nowadays. It was nice for him when Kim, his granddaughter, turned up out of the blue a few years ago. There's a bit of a mystery there which I haven't got to the bottom of yet.' Her expression said that finding this out was an ongoing project. 'I don't know where she'd been living before, but her visits seem to put a twinkle in his eye. He absolutely dotes on her. It's good that he has one visitor at least. A person can go a bit odd when they live alone, especially men . . .'

'Tracey Stubbs at number nine. What do you know about her?'

Ma gave her second sniff of the evening. 'She's got three kids under ten and another due imminently. All from different fathers. Must do nicely on the Child Benefit, though not enough to keep them in those fancy trainers she kits them out in.'

'Are you saying she's some sort of prostitute to be able to afford them?'

His ma pursed her lips and told him tartly, 'I'm saying nothing of the sort. That'd be slander. You're meant to be the policeman of the family – why don't you ask her? All I'm saying is that the girl should learn to keep her legs together. Always had poor taste in men, right from a youngster. She was always hanging round the streets, flirting with the boys. Could see where she was heading even then, even though she was quite bright. Didn't apply herself. Her mum lives around the corner. Nice a woman as you'd find. Tracey's been a trial to her. Too soft with the girl. I mean, look how Tracey turned out. Though to give the girl her due, she does work part time and the children are always well turned out. Does an evening job at the supermarket. Her mother looks after the kids.'

Rafferty, recalling his youth and his widowed ma's endless struggles to make ends meet, thought he'd ask her what she knew about Malcolm The Enforcer Forbes.

'Did you ever borrow money from him, Ma? Or from his father before him?'

His ma shook her head. 'No. But sometimes I was so desperate that I was tempted. But I'd heard how violent the Forbeses, father and son, and their collectors could be if you couldn't pay. We did without instead. Better, I thought, to do that than live in fear of the knock on the door.'

Though there had been a fair amount of that, too, as Rafferty remembered. Plenty of times they'd had to keep quiet and hide out of sight of the windows when the tally man called round for his money.

'The old man's retired now. His son has the complete running of the business. He's a real chip off the old block. Or so I hear.'

Ma made some more tea and said as she sat down again, 'And now that I've sorted out your suspects for you, tell me your own news. Have you and Abra settled on a wedding date yet?'

'We thought of May.'

'May? You can't get married in May. It's the unluckiest month of the year to wed. "Marry in May and you'll rue the day". Surely you know that?'

Bemused, Rafferty shook his head. Keen to transfer blame, he said, 'It was Abra's idea.'

Ma tutted. 'What does she know at her age? June's much

the better month. You tell her from me. You want to talk her out of May, son. No point in starting married life with the fates against you. Asking for trouble.'

As Rafferty had already had one taste of what tempting the fates could do that day, he wasn't inclined to argue. Disgruntled that the one thing they'd managed to agree on – the month of their wedding – now looked kicked into touch, Rafferty, after he left his ma's house, drove to the Chinese takeaway to pick up the food he'd rung through an order for earlier, his ma's colourful and highly prejudiced descriptions of most of the main suspects chasing each other around in his head. Wait till he told Llewellyn.

Five

It was late by now, getting on for ten o'clock, and Rafferty was too tired for much more than the briefest civility to Harry Chan, the takeaway's owner.

As he waited for Harry to bring his order, he ruminated on the day's developments. Was Ma's description of the suspects they so far had, accurate? Ma wasn't beyond exaggeration to improve a tale. Had Jaws Harrison gone into the alley for the reason he had surmised – that of gaining access to the homes of the debtors who left front door knocks unanswered? Or had he had another reason for sneaking around the back alley?

The weather was still cold and damp and though the rain had eased off markedly, the wind had turned even more blustery with evening. Rafferty was glad to get back in the car and head home to Abra.

When he reached the flat, he took off his still damp raincoat and hung it in the hall above the radiator, hoping it would be dry by morning. He paused for a few seconds to admire the newly-decorated hallway; he'd done a good job, even if he said so himself. Taupe walls with white woodwork. It still looked smart, though if Abra was still keen on buying a house as she'd said that morning, he supposed it would be back to square one on the decorating front. He breathed in on a sigh, opened the living room door and said hello to Abra.

He found her once again deep in her piles of bride and wedding magazines. What extravagance was she planning now? he wondered as he took in her bent head. The Philharmonic Orchestra for the reception? A vintage Rolls Royce to ferry her to the ceremony? He wished he knew how to get her down off her rose pink cloud of romance. It seemed to be taking her over.

Abra looked up briefly from her study of tiaras. 'Hi, Joe,' she said. 'You're late. Had a good day?'

'Not so's you'd notice. I've a murder case to solve on top of the muggings. Bloke called Jaws Harrison was killed. A collector for a local loan shark.'

Abra's lips turned down. 'I suppose that means you're going to be late every night for weeks. When are we supposed to be getting on with planning our wedding?'

Oh God, thought Rafferty. Not that again. Can't I have some peace? 'It's my job, sweetheart,' he said placatingly. 'I've no choice. And my income will help pay for the wedding you've set your heart on.'

'Will it, though, when you never seem to have time to discuss it? I seem to be the only one interested in our wedding.'

'Now that's not true. You know it's not. Please don't start. Not tonight. I'm bushed. I'll go and dish up.'

Abra followed him into the kitchen, seemingly determined to carry on the wedding conversation. He told her what his ma had said about a May wedding, thinking to get all of the bad news out of the way in one go; that way, maybe he could spend what remained of the evening in peace. 'She didn't think much of the idea, sweetheart. Said something about marrying in May and rueing the day.'

'Superstitious nonsense,' was Abra's forthright response. She seemed to be on a roll with her dissatisfaction with the Rafferty family. 'I seem to recall something similar about marrying on a Saturday, though that doesn't stop thousands getting married on that day every year.'

'Maybe. Though it would go a long way to explaining the divorce statistics.'

'Not necessarily. People have been getting married on a Saturday for generations. The only thing that goes a long way to explaining the divorce statistics is the fact that so many people nowadays don't stick at their marriages.' She smiled suddenly and Rafferty knew he'd been let off the May hook. 'But this is the only marriage I want.'

'It's the only one *I* want, too,' Rafferty said. It was true enough. He certainly hadn't wanted his first marriage to Angie, but an unexpected pregnancy had rather hastened things along on the marital front with that one. Just his luck she'd lost the baby after the wedding rather than before. Angie was dead now, leaving him with a burden of guilt at her passing. But he'd been a widower long enough. And this time he was marrying for the right reasons, he knew that, in spite of all this silliness they were currently going through over the wedding arrangements.

'Let's make it June, Abra, for the sake of peace. You know Ma will have plenty to say at the merest hint of a squabble between us if we stick to a May wedding. She'll tell us we tempted the fates.'

'Go on then. May, June – what does it matter?' she said crossly. 'I just want to get the important things settled, so I'll bow to your ma's superstitious beliefs on that one. June it is. But you needn't think your mother is going to influence all our decisions about the wedding. It's our day, not hers.'

'Indeed it is. And so I'll tell her if she comes up with any more superstitions or old wives' tales.'

'Though it's no good settling on the date unless we also settle on the place.'

Rafferty grinned. 'Ma's got firm opinions on that and all. But you know that. She has her heart set on Father Kelly marrying us in St Boniface.'

'I rather fancied one of the local stately homes. But I rang them all today. They're very popular so are booked up months ahead. So, given that I haven't got that option, I can agree to St Boniface as long as I'm not expected to learn a lot of religious claptrap in the weeks leading up to the wedding.'

Abra, unlike Rafferty, wasn't a Catholic. Not even a lapsed one. So Rafferty, suspecting the opposite, crossed his fingers behind his back as he told her, 'I think you'll find Father Kelly can be an obliging sort. And more than understanding.' With all his vices, he had to be. 'You were a bit out of it at the time, but he came up trumps when you lost little Joey early and insisted you wanted him christened.' Abra had miscarried their first child some months before in the early stages of pregnancy. 'If it hadn't been for him the christening wouldn't have happened.'

'I know that. I'm not stupid, Joe.'

'OK. So that's two of the majors sorted. Now for the guest list.' Two out of three things going his way wasn't bad for one evening, Rafferty mused, particularly given the mood Abra had worked herself into by the time he arrived home. Perhaps he was pushing his luck in going for the hat trick.

And so it proved. Abra dug her heels in over the invitees.

'Why on earth do you want all these people to attend?' Rafferty asked as he scanned the list of names. 'I've never met most of them.'

'That's because you spend so much of your time at work,' Abra pointed out. 'Besides, you've been married before. I haven't. I bet your first wife insisted on a big wedding and got her own way.'

As this was true, Rafferty didn't have much of an argument. It was no good lying to Abra. She had a way of knowing when he wasn't telling the truth. She was like his ma in that respect. Instead, he tried a more sneaky tactic. 'I wanted our marriage to be a more intimate occasion,' he began. 'Small and exclusive.' It sounded horribly pretentious put like that, but he didn't know how else to express what seemed to be his fast fading hopes of saving some money on the nuptials.

'What's the point of our big day being so small and insignificant? I want to *feel* married with the good wishes of everyone I know. I want it to be a real celebration of our love.'

Sneaky, bringing emotions into it when he was trying to concentrate on practicalities. But he was sensible enough to recognize that this was one argument he wasn't going to win, so he gave in gracefully. 'Did you manage to get anything else sorted today?'

Abra nodded. 'I beat the caterer's price down and I found a photographer a friend used for her wedding who did a great job for less than the others quoted.' She pulled a face. 'Though he wouldn't commit to a firm booking. Said he was provisionally booked throughout next summer.'

Rafferty, still hoping for a bit of peace for what remained of the evening, said, 'Don't worry, Abracadabra. We'll find someone. It's early days yet. I'll bring the food through if you do the honours on the drinks front.'

'Changing the subject, Joe? There's still loads more to sort out.'

'Not at all. Just feeding the inner man. The groom can wait a while.'

'OK. I can take a hint. We'll leave any more decisions till later in the week. I'll get those drinks.'

Rafferty smiled to himself as he made for the living room, pleased the trials of wedding arrangements would take a back seat for what remained of the evening.

Rafferty had several times had dealings with Malcolm Forbes. He'd been warned on a couple of occasions about intimidating his debtors who failed to pay their debts on time. The debtors, of course, always refused to press charges when the neighbours called the police, for fear that worse would follow. With the astronomical interest rates that Forbes charged, Rafferty was amazed that *any* of his clients managed to keep up their payments.

The weather had changed for the better; gone was the heavy rain and wind of yesterday. The pawnshop behind which Forbes operated his loan company was in Elmhurst High Street sandwiched between a charity shop and an independent butcher's. It looked reasonably smart with the morning sun glinting off its black paintwork and the three golden coloured balls that were the pawnbrokers' trademark.

'A grubby business, pawnbroking,' Rafferty remarked as they crossed the road to the shop, having parked down a side street.

'It's not as grubby as it once was,' Llewellyn commented. 'A lot of them are moving upmarket and trying to appeal to the cash-poor middle classes. Quite successfully I believe.'

'Me, I've always wondered about the three balls. Why do all pawnbrokers use them? Why not two balls? Or none at all?' Rafferty mused as he gazed in the window. It was full of watches and jewellery; mostly cheap stuff, though one or two of the engagement rings appeared more expensive, as if they had been bought in happier times when money wasn't a problem.

Needless to say, Llewellyn had an answer for his musing.

'They're a relic from fifteenth-century Florence when the Medici family of bankers had the image as their coat of arms. Did you know that pawnbroking goes back three thousand years to the Chinese?'

Rafferty didn't. And to forestall the longer lecture that he sensed was about to be delivered, he opened the door to the shop. A bell attached to the frame rang out a loud warning as Rafferty entered. The single member of staff sat caged behind a protective grille. His assessing glance showed he had got their measure, but Rafferty brought out his warrant card just the same. He introduced himself and Llewellyn and asked, 'Is Mr Forbes in? We'd like a word.'

The assistant, a thin man of around fifty, with a long, hangdog face, abandoned the racing pages of his newspaper, hopped down from his stool and said, 'I'll just see if he's available.' He knocked on a door at the back of the shop and disappeared. He came back in thirty seconds and opened up a door in the grille for them to pass through.

Malcolm Forbes was sitting behind a shabby desk that looked as if it might have formed part of his early stock; the low-key nature of the furnishings, nothing over the top or showy to fuel the punters' resentment, gave out the message that he was running a service that barely ticked over. A much-needed service for those down on their luck rather than a profiteering racket with a serial usurer at its head.

'Ah, Inspector Rafferty. I learned from the officer you sent to see me yesterday that you were in charge of the murder investigation. John Harrison's a sad loss.' This was said with a suitably mournful demeanour. Then, mock mourning over, it was business as usual as he asked, 'How's the case going? Are you anywhere near catching the scum who killed him?'

'The investigation is progressing as expected, Mr Forbes,' Rafferty told him, keeping his feelings in check. He'd never liked Forbes. The man was an overbearing bully. It went against the grain to have to be polite to him. 'All the residents of the street adjoining the alley where he was found have been questioned and will be so again.'

Forbes was a big man, though clearly not in *every* sense, given his barely concealed lack of interest in the late John Harrison. He had a jowly red face that could have looked jolly but for the mean grey eyes. Still, there was a surface bonhomie there. But scratch the surface and pretty soon the real Forbes emerged; the small town thug who thought he was Mr Big.

Rafferty's teeth grated together as he awaited some derogatory comment.

But today, with them, Forbes was clearly in a magnanimous mood. He invited them to sit down and asked how he could help.

With difficulty, they squeezed on to two narrow chairs wedged under the barred rear window. 'We wondered what you could tell us about the victim,' Rafferty began. 'Whether anything about him can have contributed to his death.'

Forbes frowned, turning his beetling brows into a monobrow. 'But surely this was just another mugging like the other two cases?' The welcoming smile vanished with his question to be replaced by the ferocious scowl of the true thug. His expression made clear that no one damaged his business or his employees and got away with it. *He* was the one who doled out the violence and threats of violence. It made Rafferty hope that they caught the perpetrator before Forbes did: he wouldn't like to be on the receiving end of Forbes's retribution.

'Had the late Mr Harrison worked for you for long?' Rafferty asked.

'Eighteen months or thereabouts. I can check my records if you like.' It was a tight squeeze in the small office as he swivelled his chair around towards a filing cabinet, reached for a file and handed it over.

'Tell me, had any of your clients made threats against him?'

Forbes gave a cynical laugh. 'Most of them I should think, at one time or another. Our client base is not of the brightest and they relieve their anger at being expected to repay their loans by making empty threats. They're happy enough to borrow money from me, but less happy when they're asked to start paying the instalments. Such threats are part and parcel of the job. But I know how to deal with them. Let the punters backslide once and they'll expect to be able to do it again. The trick is not to let them backslide at all. Gentle persuasion usually does the trick.' Forbes's irony was heavy-handed and cynical. The persuasion was only gentle if broken arms and smashed jaws came into that category. 'Nothing has ever come of any of their threats.'

'Until now,' Rafferty reminded him. Though, as yet, they had no clear evidence apart from their close proximity to the alley to point to any one of Harrison's collectees having murdered him. 'I'll need to know the names of those who issued the threats. One of them might be Mr Harrison's murderer.'

Forbes leaned back in his chair and gazed at him from under his thick, black brows. 'I doubt it. Weak old men and stupid women, most of them. Harrison was a strong man. A big, muscular man. It would take, I would have thought, someone with a strength greater than their threat to kill him.'

'Maybe so. But we have to investigate every avenue. One of them will lead us to the murderer.'

Rafferty glanced quickly through John Harrison's staff file. There wasn't much of it; references about good behaviour and a pleasing disposition were unlikely to be required in Forbes's business. A full set of muscles and an intimidating manner provided all the references required. He hefted Harrison's file and asked, 'OK if we take this?'

Forbes gave a shrug of acquiescence.

Rafferty handed Harrison's file to Llewellyn and reminded Forbes, 'About those threats. If I can have some names?'

Forbes shrugged his meaty shoulders. 'As I said, threats are an occupational hazard. I only hear about them if my collectors feel something might come of them.'

'And did Mr Harrison mention any such threats?'

'One or two.' Forbes shifted in his chair and it creaked in protest. It was a big, sturdy executive chair, but it clearly found Forbes's weight at the edge of its limits. 'A couple of little old ladies who were more feisty than usual, that's all. Nothing to frighten a grown man. He only told me about them because he thought they were amusing. Names of Mrs Noades and Miss Peterson.'

Rafferty did a quick check of his memory banks. Neither of the women lived on Primrose Avenue. 'So nobody from Primrose Avenue threatened him?'

'Not to my knowledge. If they did, he didn't see fit to mention it to me.' Forbes rose from his chair, his bulk seemed to fill a good half of the cramped office. 'If that's all?'

Rafferty nodded, glad he wasn't on the receiving end of intimidation from such a man. It was clear there was little else to be gained by prolonging the conversation. 'We'll see ourselves out.'

'All right?' the assistant asked as they came through the door.

Rafferty nodded and thanked him.

The assistant let them out through the grille. And once they were back on the street, Rafferty said, 'Mr Forbes wasn't too chatty, was he, seeing as it's one of his staff who's dead. Reckon he intends to find out who killed Harrison himself and mete out his own punishment?'

'It would certainly fit his profile.'

'Or maybe he's hiding something else?'

'What, do you think he might have had something to do with Mr Harrison's death?'

'I don't know. Why would he? The only reason I can think of is if Harrison was helping himself to some of the money he collected and Forbes found out about it.'

It was another chilly day. Rafferty said, 'Come on, let's step on it and get back to the car. My feet are like blocks of ice.'

They increased their pace, rounded the corner, and made for the car.

'But would he murder Harrison if so?' Llewellyn mused out loud on Rafferty's previous point. 'Rather a drastic way of teaching someone a lesson.'

'Mmm. Admittedly, it would be difficult to learn that or any other lesson when you're dead. But maybe Forbes would be more concerned with keeping up his reputation as a man not to be crossed. Collectors like Harrison are probably ten a penny. Nothing like throwing your weight about and getting paid for it. It must be a nice little number for a certain type of man.'

Rafferty opened the car door and got in, glad to get out of the wind. He started the engine and turned the heater up to its maximum setting, willing it to kick in quickly. 'Though if Forbes had anything to do with Harrison's murder, I reckon we'll be the last to hear. Like the mafia's code of *omertà*, that sort of information is unlikely to be for our ears.' He checked the mirror and pulled out. 'Let's get back. Maybe something new has come in.'

But once back at the station, there was no revelatory news awaiting them; just more of the labour-intensive paperwork that was so familiar. And Superintendent Bradley demanding a progress report. He coerced Rafferty along to his office and closed the door firmly behind them.

'So what's doing on the murder front? You must have some suspects, but?' he said as he sat behind his massive desk.

'We have a number of suspects,' Rafferty told him as he studied the array of photographs of Bradley cosying up to the great and good on the wall behind his desk. 'Half the residents of Primrose Avenue had the opportunity to kill Harrison and all of *them* had good reasons to murder him.'

'Anyone specific in mind?'

'Not yet. It's early days. But there are several youths who'll bear closer scrutiny.'

Bradley nodded. 'I shall want a report by the end of the day. And not one of your usual scrimped efforts. And no getting Llewellyn to do it for you. You're the investigating officer. Remember it.'

If only I could forget, thought Rafferty as the super let him go. With a succession of long days I'm not going to be flavour of the month with Abra. Worse, the evenings alone would give her even more opportunity to think of novel ways of overspending.

'I think we should take a thorough look through Harrison's home,' Rafferty said when he returned to his office. He sat down and leaned back in his chair away from the incessant paperwork. Annie Pulman had earlier been persuaded to identify the body; they'd dropped her back home on their way to interview Malcolm Forbes. 'If he was helping himself to some of the cash from his collections that's where we'd find it. It's not as if he'd be likely to put it in a bank or building society.' He glanced down at the high-piled paperwork the house-to-house had produced and sighed. Then his emotions rose at the realization that the visit to Jaws Harrison's place would enable him to put off fighting his way through it for a while. And if they found a stack of cash or anything else of interest there, the paperwork could be put off for even longer as they chased evidence against Forbes in the role of murderer.

'It's still possible we're on the wrong scent and that some-one had reason other than debt to want him dead.'

'We've no evidence for that,' Llewellyn pointed out. 'The facts point the other way. Few enough could have had the opportunity to kill him down that alleyway. The killer would surely have been seen either going in or coming out, no matter what motive they might have had.'

'Maybe, but we've only the word of Tony Moran for that. The other three yobbos in their little gang are sticking pretty much to their "no comment" stance, though at least Jake Sterling backed up Moran about the identities of the three women who left the avenue that afternoon. And no one else has so far come forward with any evidence.'

In spite of what Llewellyn said, it was certainly a possi-bility that someone other than one of the Primrose Avenue residents had killed Harrison, especially when the late Harrison's personality was taken into the equation. He spent his life throwing his weight about and threatening those in no position to retaliate; maybe he'd met his match, and his murderer had been someone whose visit to the avenue Moran had preferred not to mention. Like Malcolm Forbes, for instance.

Annie Pulman answered the door. She looked surprised to see them again so soon. Given her so recent bereavement, her tears seemed to have dried up remarkably quickly after identifying John Harrison's body. Clearly not cut out to play the grieving widow for long.

Rafferty explained the reason for their visit. Annie Pulman stared at him with a hostile expression for several seconds, but then she stood aside to let them pass.

'Isn't it enough that my John's dead,' her plaintive voice followed after them up the stairs and down the hallway, 'without going through his things? You're just in time anyway. I was getting his clothes and stuff packed to take up the second-hand shop.'

It had been one day since Harrison's murder; clearly she hadn't let grief come between her and the prospect of making some money from his possessions.

As he and Llewellyn went through the bags of Harrison's clothes, Rafferty questioned the woman.

'Were you happy together?' he asked. Though, to judge from a bruise around her eye that had just started to come up, the pair couldn't have been love's young dream or anything like it.

'We did all right.'

The bruise contradicted her claim. So here was another who had reason to harbour resentment, hatred even, of Jaws Harrison. He supposed it was too much to expect Harrison to have left his bullying tendencies the other side of his front door.

Rafferty, still considering the possibility that someone other than their current crop of suspects had killed him, questioned her about her whereabouts on the day of the murder and received evasive replies.

'What are you asking me for? I didn't kill him. I told you, we did all right. I had no reason to wish him dead. I won't even be able to stay here in the flat as I can't afford the rent on my own. Do you think I want the trouble of moving so soon after I've lost John?'

Not that he thought it likely she'd trailed Harrison all the way to Primrose Avenue – he asked and she claimed not to have a car or anyone close from whom she could borrow one. He'd get Uniformed to check with the Swansea records and amongst the neighbours.

'You must know some of his friends and acquaintances. If you could let me have their names and addresses?'

'He didn't have many friends. Apart from me, he was pretty much a loner. He had a few acquaintances, but I don't know much about them. Only their first names. I've no idea where they live.'

He managed to get this small stock of information from her. Then they left her alone and went into the bedroom she'd shared with Harrison.

To Rafferty's surprise, they found a notebook hidden at the back of one of the drawers in the bedroom chest of drawers. To his frustration, the notes seemed to have been written in some sort of code. He couldn't make head nor tail of it anyway. They also found a stack of cash. It came to a thousand pounds. Had the money come from thieving from Forbes? Or had Harrison made some money on the side from blackmail? He was certainly in the right job for ferreting out secrets, lurking around back alleys as he did. He showed the notebook to Annie Pulman and asked if she knew anything about it. She denied it.

'What's in it, then?' she wanted to know. 'If it was John's then that means it's mine now. I was his common law wife.'

There's no such thing in law, Rafferty felt like telling her, not liking her eager grasp of the so recently deceased Harrison's possessions. But he restrained the urge. There was little point in telling her that unless Harrison had made a will, which seemed doubtful, then she was unlikely to receive any of his belongings. Not, he suspected, that the finer points of the Intestacy Law would trouble her. She had already sorted through her lover's clothes to sell them. Anything of value may well have already been pawned or sold. He doubted, looking round the cheaply furnished flat, that there could have been much of any value. She was welcome to it as far as he was concerned. But he was taking the notebook, as he told her. And the money. As was to be expected, she made far more of a protest about this when he told her of its existence. But as she was unable to tell him how Harrison had come by such a sum of money, he insisted on taking it as evidence. Silently, he wrote her out a receipt.

Not realizing it could hold some value for her, she had no real interest in the notebook. He doubted it would have meant more to her than it did to him. If the notebook did indeed contain the names of those Harrison could have been black-mailing it was unlikely the dead man would have shared any information about them with Annie Pulman. He'd have kept that and the money he prised out of his victims strictly to himself.

There was nothing else of interest in the flat. Before they left, Rafferty asked her again where she had been on the afternoon of the murder. Clearly, she'd thought better of her earlier hasty and evasive replies and said, 'I was at my mum's, wasn't I? It was my day off and I thought I'd go round and see her. I stayed for lunch and tea. I got back around six.'

They obtained her mother's name and address after a little effort and told her they'd check with Mrs Pulman. They'd check with her mother's neighbours also, Rafferty decided, seeing as he didn't think it beyond the realms of possibility that Annie Pulman wasn't a stranger to lies when it suited her and would prime her mother with them by phone as soon as they had left.

'This notebook adds an extra dimension to the case,' Rafferty confided to Llewellyn as they left Annie Pulman's flat. 'Looks like our late lamented could have been a blackmailer. Shame the blasted thing's written in some weird schoolboy code.'

'May I have a look?'

Rafferty nodded and handed the notebook over. But even though he needed to understand the mystery of its contents he couldn't help a little leap of pleasure when Llewellyn also proved incapable of making anything of it.

Llewellyn went to hand it back, but Rafferty told him to hang on to it. 'Work on it,' he told him. 'I'm no great shakes at word puzzles. I'm sure your great brain will have better luck than mine in figuring out what it says.'

Six

The answer to the question of the identity of their 'suited and booted' mystery man whom Tony Moran saw enter Tracey Stubbs's house on Primrose Avenue on the afternoon of Jaws Harrison's murder was answered later that day when they resumed the questioning of the residents. The mystery man turned out to be a collector for a rival firm of loan sharks, as they discovered when they questioned Tracey Stubbs.

Ms Stubbs was a young woman in her mid-twenties with a nose stud and an assortment of tattoos decorating her bare shoulders and midriff. Her hair was worn in a longer version of the spikes of Jake Sterling and his cohorts. In spite of her rather aggressive looking style, she proved helpful.

'You say you didn't obtain your loan from Malcolm Forbes?' Strangely, she had been on the list Forbes had supplied. Though perhaps the business took less trouble in keeping their paperwork straight than they did in keeping the money coming in.

Tracey Stubbs shook her head. 'I did apply, but then I read a small ad in the local paper and got a loan from them instead.'

Rafferty strained to hear above the children shouting in the other room; it seemed as if Ms Stubbs had half the neighbourhood children in the house. They were running up and downstairs, whooping and yelling, but Tracey Stubbs didn't bat an eyelid or even admonish them. The house was as untidy as only a houseful of kids could make it, with skates and footballs and bikes left where they'd been dropped. Tracey had made a half-hearted attempt to tidy after their arrival, but it had made little difference to the mess and she'd quickly abandoned it, clearly seeing her efforts as a forlorn attempt to create order out of chaos.

'Do you still have the ad?' he asked. If she had got a loan out from another firm it was possible that this other collector and Jaws Harrison had run into one another. They might learn something useful from this other firm.

'I think so.' She looked around vaguely, then headed over to an overflowing brass magazine rack. After hunting through various local free sheets, TV listings and celebrity magazines, she found the paper she was looking for and handed it over. 'I ringed the ad.'

Rafferty studied it. It was the usual cajoling come-on of such things, with 'Debt Problems?' at the top of the ad in a bold heading and a sympathetic portrayal of how helpful they could be to those at the end of their tether. Like Forbes, this loan shark wouldn't be so sympathetic if one of their customers failed on the paying front. There was what looked like a mobile phone number as well as a post office box number for replies, which would have immediately put Rafferty on the alert if he was looking for a loan – which, with the wedding, he well might be in the near future. 'All right if I take this?' he asked.

Tracey nodded. 'Though I don't know what use it can be to you as it's a different firm of moneylenders to the one the dead bloke collected for. I know Malcolm Forbes operates out of his shop on the High Street. After I'd applied, but before I signed up for a loan with him, I heard bad things about him and how he operates from some of the neighbours, so I changed my mind about going to him for a loan.'

Rafferty thought it likely the firm she'd opted for instead carried out its business in a similar way to Forbes. 'Do you recall the name of the people who gave you a loan?'

'Not off the top of my head. I can probably find the paperwork.' She looked vaguely around the untidy living room and made a half-hearted attempt to go through a drawer in the sideboard.

Her search didn't look promising, so Rafferty said, 'Don't worry. I'm sure we can find the details for ourselves. Tell me, do you go to the offices of the people who gave you the loan to make the payments or do they come and collect?'

'They call every week on a Friday.'

'So what time did they call this week?'

'Around three fifteen. They generally call in the afternoon after I've collected the younger kids from play school.'

Once back outside on the pavement, Rafferty gave Llewellyn the newspaper. He jabbed his finger at the circled ad and said, 'Check these people out. It's possible their collector saw something. Got to be pretty sharp to do their job. Unlike the residents of Primrose Avenue, we can hope he has no axe to grind, so we may get something approaching the truth if he knows anything.'

Llewellyn looked strangely pleased with himself when he returned to the station and Rafferty's office.

'Don't tell me Lizzie Green goosed you?' Rafferty asked as he glanced up. 'Lucky man.'

'No. I hope she knows better than to goose a sergeant. It's something much better. It might amuse you, too. Or maybe not. As you asked, I've been checking out the firm of loan sharks from whom Tracey Stubbs took out a loan. I found out their details from the local sorting office. Their offices are here in Elmhurst and are housed in Blythe's Estate Agents.'

'No.' Rafferty groaned. 'Don't tell me—'

'I'm afraid so. It seems your cousin Nigel Blythe has branched out from that estate agency of his.'

Rafferty scowled. What was Nigel doing getting involved in moneylending? Most of the time he was hard-pressed to keep himself in the style to which he had become accustomed, never mind lending cash to perfect strangers. Had he come into money? Rafferty doubted it. He would surely have heard via the family grapevine if so.

Nigel was the family pariah, even more so than Rafferty as a copper was, probably because, as an estate agent, he was a bent one. Rafferty's family – some of them, anyway – would have preferred Rafferty to be a bent copper, though as a straight police officer, he earned a grudging respect.

Doubtless it was the prospect of easy money and high interest rates that had attracted Nigel to the loan sharking business. Always, even as a lad, he'd had an eye for the main chance and would somehow manage to cheat the other school kids out of their dinner money. He and Rafferty had never been particularly close. It was more a toleration than anything else, a toleration that had increased with the years when both, in their different ways, had broken out from the family's usual pursuits of working in the building trade, Rafferty as a policeman and Nigel as an estate agent. Then their paths had also crossed at family weddings, christenings and funerals and in several of Rafferty's cases over the years. They both had secrets about the other which sometimes gave a little leeway one way or the other.

'So what did Nigel have to say for himself? You have seen him, I take it?'

'No. I thought I'd save that particular treat for you, though I did telephone him.'

'Did he give you the name of his collector who called on Tracey Stubbs?'

'He did indeed. The collector was none other than Mr Blythe himself. It seems his regular collector isn't as regular or dependable as Mr Blythe would like, so he was forced to do that day's rounds himself.'

Probably couldn't bring himself to trust someone else when it came to collecting his money, thought Rafferty. Nigel thought everyone was as bent as he was. This was a turn up and no mistake. 'And did our Nigel have anything helpful to say?'

'The conversation went much as I expected. Mr Blythe claims he saw nothing untoward, though he did admit to seeing John Harrison enter the alley. He'd apparently been keeping him in view so he didn't bump into him. I gather there had been a little unpleasantness between Mr Forbes's collector and the one Mr Blythe used. A certain intimidation over whose "turf" it was, I gather.'

Nigel was taking a risk trying to muscle in on Forbes The Enforcer's patch. It wasn't like Nigel to put his handsome face and even handsomer suits at risk from fisticuffs or worse. Nigel was more likely to put a million miles and a thousand smarms between himself and such dangers. So had the lure of filthy lucre changed his mind? It was the only thing likely to, in Rafferty's judgement.

'I think I'll go and speak to Mr Blythe myself.' He glanced at the clock. 'It's too late to catch him now. He'll probably be out on the town with one of his lady friends. 'I'll have to try tomorrow. Maybe he'll tell me more than he told you.'

'Do you really think so?'

Rafferty didn't. Knowing Nigel, or Jerry Kelly as was, the name with which he had been bestowed at birth and which he had discarded along with his lowly roots, he would be more likely to tell him even less than he'd confided to Llewellyn. Still, it would be worth it to get a feel for his cousin's latest entrepreneurial enterprise. He wondered who Nigel used as his regular collector down Primrose Avenue. He also wondered how long his latest business venture had been going. It couldn't have been long; otherwise he would surely have heard of it.

'Good work, Daff,' he said. 'Isn't it amazing what worms come out of the ground when you do a bit of digging?'

Llewellyn, who knew this particular worm quite well, gave a nod.

'Let's speak to Mr Jenkins at number eleven next,' Rafferty said. 'We've just got time to fit him in.'

A young blonde woman in her early twenties answered when they knocked on Jim Jenkins's door to follow up the house-to-house interviews. Mr Jenkins made brief introductions.

'This is my granddaughter, Kim.'

Kim smiled, kissed her grandfather and said, 'I'll leave you to it, Pops. And thanks again.'

'Get along with you girl. What are granddads for?' In spite of his disclaimer, he looked pleased, the crêpey skin around his blue eyes crinkled even more as he patted her hand affectionately.

As she passed Rafferty, she said in a low murmur, 'Go easy on him, Inspector. He's neither a young nor a well man.'

Rafferty could see that Jim Jenkins moved with difficulty around his living room, hanging on to the table and a chair back as he settled himself into a clean but neatly patched armchair after insisting on seeing his granddaughter out. Invited to sit down, Rafferty did so. Llewellyn perched beside him.

'I understand, sir, that you aren't numbered amongst those who took out a loan with Malcolm Forbes's company?'

'Certainly not. I don't believe in taking out loans. "Neither a borrower nor a lender be" was what my old mum taught me and it's held me in good stead throughout my life.'

Although looking well over ninety and far from sprightly, Jim Jenkins's voice was strong and held the timbre of command. Rafferty guessed from the few pictures of old soldiers hanging on the walls that Jim Jenkins was a World War Two veteran. He could just glimpse what must be a chestful of medals through the partly open drawer of the old Welsh dresser. Rafferty nodded at the photos and asked, 'Which regiment were you in, sir?'

'Royal Marines, young man. But I rarely talk about my war experiences. It was all a very long time ago. Now, tell me how I can help you.'

Rafferty nodded. 'I know you told the house-to-house team that you saw nothing on the day Mr Harrison was murdered, but I wondered if you might have heard anything that you've since remembered. A cry or a scuffle. Anything, no matter how trivial you might think it.'

'My faculties aren't what they were, Inspector. I heard nothing out of the ordinary. Friday was just another day to be got through to me until the policeman knocked on my back door. I'm not one of those forever peering through the curtains to see what the neighbours are up to. I keep myself to myself. The neighbourhood isn't what it was when my late wife and I bought this house.'

He didn't add 'neither are the neighbours', but he might as well have done.

'I gather you lent one of the neighbours, a Mr Eric Lewis, your hedge-trimmer?'

'That's correct. He kept it for weeks. Most annoying as I had my own hedges to trim. I thought I'd have to ask him for it back. I was going to, but with all the rumpus this man Harrison's death has caused, it went out of my mind. I like to keep a tidy garden, you see.'

Rafferty did see. In spite of his age and poor mobility, Jim Jenkins's garden was the best-kept in the street and was a symbol of the neighbourhood's previous standards whilst most of the other gardens only hinted at its decline.

'One of my officers picked up your hedge-trimmer from

the alley where Eric Lewis dropped it when he stumbled over the body. It's currently undergoing forensic tests. I'll make sure it's returned to you as soon as they're completed.'

Mr Jenkins thanked him.

'Did you know the dead man?' Llewellyn asked.

'Not to speak to. He didn't strike me as the type willing to pass the time of day, especially not with an old man like me. I nodded to him when I saw him, whether or not he displayed a similar courtesy. But I knew of him. My next-door neighbour, Mrs Parker, told me she took out a loan with the dead man's firm. I think she's lived to regret it. I've several times seen him knock on her door. She didn't even trouble to keep her borrowing secret as one would in my day. She told me all about it. She's always catching me over the garden fence to share the latest gossip. It's getting so I'm reluctant to go out there. She's a very difficult woman to get away from unless one is rude. So I knew what he did. I just didn't make use of his services.'

Poor Jim Jenkins, thought Rafferty. What a come down for an old soldier. Caught between a determined gossip for a neighbour on one side and a horde of unruly kids on the other. Between the two he couldn't get a lot of peace. No wonder he tried to keep himself to himself. With limited success, it seemed, if Mrs Emily Parker had anything to do with it.

It was clear Jim Jenkins couldn't help them further. Rafferty got up and bade the old man goodbye as he handed him his card. 'If you remember anything, anything at all, perhaps you'd give me a call.'

'Certainly I'll give you a call, but I'd prefer to speak to you face to face if I remember anything. I don't like telephones. I find them a trial since my hearing started to fail.' He went to heave himself out of his chair with the aid of a stick, but Rafferty forestalled him.

'Please don't trouble. We can see ourselves out.'

'It's no trouble. As well as not being a borrower, my mother also instilled good manners into me. I'm still able to follow the basic courtesies.' By now, he had prised himself out of his chair and stood on uncertain legs like a newborn foal, precariously balanced by the use of a stick. 'The day I can't manage the civilities is the day they carry me out of here in my box.'

As they made for the car, Llewellyn returned to an earlier topic of conversation. 'Do you really think you'll learn anything from Mr Blythe?'

'Probably not. He's already putting his health on the line by setting up in competition with Forbes. He's unlikely to be able to hide behind a post office box number for very long.' They climbed in the car and buckled up. 'I know our Nigel likes the old folding stuff and lots of it, but I wouldn't have thought him likely to think a bit more of it worth a good kicking. Especially with him having such a pretty face. Still, you never know. If he saw Forbes or some other loan shark's thuggish minions besides Harrison while he was in Primrose Avenue, he might think it worth his while to let us know on the quiet, in the hope that we'll remove one of his competitors.'

Nigel grassing to his police inspector cousin sounded an unlikely event once voiced. But as he turned the car towards the station Rafferty tried to keep optimistic; maybe Nigel had turned over a new leaf and would be cooperative? He could but hope.

Seven

Jaws Harrison had been quite the enterprising fellow if blackmail *had* been his game. His entrepreneurial skills made Rafferty see he'd been sluggish in ordering his own life to his advantage. But it wasn't too late to change that. After all, cousin Nigel wasn't the only member of the family able to branch out. Wedding organizer had a certain ring to it. How difficult could it be? Maybe one day, with his own wedding organization under his belt, and if he got really fed up with the job, he could take it up full time. He was full of this idea when he got home to Abra that evening and broached it to her.

'Abra. About the wedding . . .'

Immediately, a defensive look crossed her face. 'What about it?' she asked sharply.

She sounded defensive, too. Rafferty knew that Llewellyn's wife, Maureen, had had a word with Abra, but from her tone, the word had been to no avail.

'I just wanted to see if we could compromise on some areas, that's all,' Rafferty began before Abra interrupted him.

'Like what? Do you want us to provide a wedding breakfast of cod and chips, perhaps? Or have me dressed in sackcloth with ashes decorating my hair?'

'You're being ridiculous.' They'd already had this conversation once and Rafferty had no desire to do so again. 'There's no reason to be so aggressive. It's my day too, remember.'

'I do remember. It's just that you don't seem very interested in anything to do with our wedding apart from keeping the costs to the bare minimum.'

'That's not true. But someone has to keep an eye on the money aspect. And you seem determined to make this the wedding of the decade. I saw you looking through brochures for wedding cars when I came in. So what are you thinking of booking? A vintage Rolls Royce? Or maybe you fancy a four-horse carriage?' Rafferty was aware that he was beginning to sound as aggressive as Abra. He took a deep breath and said, 'Look, sweetheart, I think doing everything is getting a bit on top of you. Why don't you leave me to organize some of the wedding arrangements?'

'Leave them to you? But you've got a murder to solve.'

'Oh, that old thing –' he shrugged – 'I've nearly got it sorted already.' Rafferty rushed on before Abra thought to question this statement. 'I meet all sorts of people in my job and have some useful contacts.'

'Yes,' Abra replied caustically. 'Thieves and murderers mostly.'

'Not all of them. You'd be surprised. I've even mixed with some titled people in my time.'

'What do you want me to do? Curtsey? Don't tell me you're going to invite some Sir Bigwig to our wedding?'

'No. The bigwigs I was thinking of have moved away. And I don't know where they are.' Well, that was true, anyway. Though Hell seemed the likeliest destination.

'You're not going to be inviting any of the brass from the job? I remember Superintendent Bradley was supposed to be going to Dafyd's wedding, but he never showed.'

'No. That was Maureen's mother getting delusions of grandeur. Not something Ma's likely to suffer from. How about your mother? Fancy mingling with the brass, does she?'

'She doesn't know any of them.'

Neither did Ma and he was happy to keep it that way. God knew what knocked-off piece of finery she might turn up in to their wedding. 'No. Definitely no brass,' Rafferty said firmly. 'I know you said you'd had no luck in getting a firm booking from your favoured photographer, but we need to get it sorted. I know a great photographer. Regularly photographs the force bigwigs.'

'I don't want a military-looking wedding, Joe, with all brass and blanko.'

'And you won't get one, my sweet. He's versatile, my man.'

'*Your* man?'

'Yes. He owes me a few favours.' He didn't, but it sounded good. Anything had to be better – and cheaper – than Abra's choice of photographer. And he was likely to get a few quid off just because photographing a wedding would provide a bit of light relief from all that brassy self-importance of the politically correct elite. He might even get the opportunity to chat up a bridesmaid or two as a bonus.

Now he thought seriously about it, he had a few other contacts who might be persuaded to do things at cost or not much more. Yes, things were starting to look a bit brighter on the wedding front. He should save himself a pretty penny. He didn't know why he hadn't suggested taking over some of the arrangements before.

One of these contacts was a manager at the swanky four-star Elmhurst Hotel. He might be persuaded to give over one of their ballrooms for the reception. After all, Rafferty had solved two murders on the Elmhurst's premises. If that wasn't good for a favour, he didn't know what was.

Yes, if he played his cards right, he should be able to save himself a packet.

Briefly, he flirted with the idea of asking his ma if she was still in contact with the tailor who specialized in high-style suits at low, low prices. But then, when he remembered the trauma he'd gone through over a previous suit in the lead-up to Llewellyn's wedding, he decided against it. Better not try to trim the costs there. But the rest was still up for grabs. Maybe some of the lads at the station knew a florist who could do the bouquets and so on for a knockdown price. If he wasn't to end up bankrupted by this wedding it was time to pull out all the stops. The predicaments of Forbes's debtors provided the required prod if prod were needed.

What else was to be arranged? He was sure Llewellyn would be able to knock out something tasteful on his computer by way of invitations. He seemed to remember him mentioning some new graphic software he'd bought. He'd become quite animated about it. A couple of hundred invitations shouldn't be beyond his tame computer nerd.

He'd nip round to The Elmhurst Hotel in the morning and have a word with the manager. Their ballrooms were as stylish as any: Edwardian with all the grandeur Abra could wish for. He just hoped the present manager didn't up sticks and move to another job between now and the wedding.

It was a contented Rafferty who settled down with Abra to enjoy the rest of their evening. Thankfully, at Rafferty's suggestion of taking over some of the arrangements, she'd mellowed, no longer able to accuse him of taking no interest in their wedding. And as they turned the pages of the holiday brochures full of exotic honeymoon destinations, Rafferty began to rack his brains to think who amongst his acquaintances had a holiday home they might be willing to let them have in lieu of a wedding present.

Rafferty set off for The Elmhurst Hotel the following morning as soon as he'd read the latest reports and before Superintendent Bradley could collar him for an update on the murder investigation.

It was a bright, sunny day and he was chirpy as he drove from the station, whistling as he made his way to The Elmhurst. He was pleased with life and his own initiative. Get The Elmhurst Hotel organized for the reception and he'd be well in Abra's good books. And if he could get the rest sorted, too, she'd think he was Mr Wonderful. He began singing 'I'm H-A-P-P-Y, I'm H-A-P-P-Y, I know I am, I'm sure I am, I'm H-A-P-P-Y.'

The manager was in the middle of sorting out a minor crisis when he arrived, but Rafferty said he was willing to wait. He gazed around the plush reception and wondered which of the ballrooms the manager would be able to let him have. Say what you liked about the Edwardians, but they knew how to turn out elegant buildings and interiors.

Twenty minutes later, with the crisis resolved and the manager now all welcoming smiles, Rafferty was quick to remind him what a stalwart policeman he had been on the occasions of the two murders that had taken place at the hotel. They proceeded in mutual reminiscence about Rafferty's cleverness and sensitivity for several minutes, then he steered the conversation from death to life and what each was doing now.

Rafferty told him he was in the middle of investigating

another murder. 'But that's not why I called to see you. I'm getting married.'

'Congratulations.'

But even as the manager mouthed the word, Rafferty caught the wary expression and he realized that it should have occurred to him that a man with three ballrooms at his disposal must have a lot of favours called in from friends and family as well as mere acquaintances. No wonder he had looked wary at the mention of the wedding word. But surely, getting the manager out of the hole into which two violent deaths had thrust him must be worth more on the favour front than just being a second cousin twice removed?

The manager tried to cover up his base, unspoken ingratitude by asking when the wedding was to be held.

Rafferty told him.

'June! One of our busiest months. Of course our ballrooms are all booked for the next eighteen months. Everyone these days has to book everything well in advance if they want the venue of their choice.'

It seemed the manager followed that old saw about the best form of defence being attack; he'd certainly got his defence in early.

Dismayed that his brightly laid plans had fallen at the first hurdle, Rafferty said, 'But you must have cancellations. Couldn't—?'

'Of course. And we've nearly as many bookings for those as we have for the wedding receptions. Weddings are big business nowadays, Inspector. Gone are the days when a couple could book up six months in advance and have their first choice. The statistics for those getting married may well be the lowest ever, but the requirements have risen. More and more people want a big wedding – the bigger the better, with no expense spared. Yes, we do very nicely out of the wedding market. It helps to keep us afloat during otherwise quiet times.'

This was something Rafferty was beginning to realize. He slunk off a few minutes later, his tail doing its best to trip him up and with his prospective alternative career as a wedding organizer killed at birth.

But he wasn't done yet. He still had high hopes over one

or two of the other arrangements he had persuaded Abra to let him take over. Of course a swish hotel like The Elmhurst would be booked up months in advance. He should have realized that for himself. He was just thankful he hadn't mentioned the possibility of booking the place to Abra. As it was, he'd already tried to pin down the usual brass photographer to a firm commitment to do the wedding, but he was playing fast and loose with him, complaining of the usual screaming brats he'd have to contend with at a wedding. Rafferty had countered with the reply that at least children's tantrums couldn't be on a par with those of the brass in mid strop. But still the man wouldn't commit himself and said he'd get back to him. With that he'd had to be content. But at least the wretch hadn't said an outright no. As for the reception venue, he'd have to come up with somewhere else unless Abra agreed to postpone the wedding for another year. But as he couldn't see that going down too well he didn't dwell on the possibility for long.

But even with The Elmhurst Hotel out of the window as a reception venue, he was still determined to wrestle control of as many of the wedding arrangements as possible from an Abra who was proving unwarrantably extravagant. He was gung-ho no longer. And Cousin Nigel was next on the agenda.

Nigel Blythe was in the private office at the estate agency he owned. This was starkly modern with black leather and chrome, the seats uncomfortably low, all the better to keep potential buyers on the premises and open to persuasion. As always, Nigel looked Italian gigolo-smart in a three-piece mauve suit and a silver-grey tie. No wonder Tony Moran had described him as a peacock. Rafferty was only surprised he'd felt such a small stir of recognition at Moran's description.

'Well, well,' Nigel greeted their arrival as he leant back in his high-backed leather executive chair. 'Look what the cat dragged in.'

'Nice to see you, too, Jerry.' Rafferty pulled up a chair and sat down.

The smile vanished from Nigel's face at Rafferty's use of

his true given name. Nigel Blythe didn't like reminders of his common name and lowly origins. But Jerry Kelly he would always remain to Rafferty, who thought Nigel shouldn't be allowed to become *too* forgetful of their shared background. Nigel preferred to pretend he had sprung, fully formed, as a smartly-dressed and suave estate agent.

Even though Rafferty knew it was unwise to antagonize his cousin if he wanted his cooperation, he couldn't help himself. Nigel's pretensions tended to rub him up the wrong way. 'I hear you've gone into the loan shark business,' he said.

'Then you hear wrong.' Nigel's handsome face, that was superficially so like Rafferty's, but so much better looking, scowled. 'I run a respectable loan firm. Nothing wrong in that.'

'I doubt if Malcolm Forbes would agree with you. I wonder if he's learned of your little business yet. I hear your men and his have had a few little contretemps at least.'

Nigel paled at the mention of Forbes's name, but he quickly regained his confidence. 'I'm sure Mr Forbes isn't frightened of a little competition.'

'I wouldn't bet on it.'

'You haven't told him, have you?'

'Would I do that?'

'I wouldn't put it past you. You're a copper and would probably be pleased if Forbes set one of his goons on me.'

'No. Not at all. And spoil that nice suit? Looks an expensive bit of shmutter.'

'It is. Anyway, there's room for all of us in the business given the high rate of personal debt in the country. Like death and taxes, it's ever with us and the number of debtors increases every year. I'm just doing my bit to help those in need.'

'What a veritable fund of benevolence you are. I must put you forward for an award.'

'You might sneer,' said Nigel, 'though I don't know why you think yourself so superior. After all, debt is something your family is familiar with.'

'And yours,' Rafferty shot back. Even as he said it, he was aware that he was being juvenile and unprofessional. But there was something about Nigel that tended to bring out the worst in him. For a moment, he thought Nigel was about to add some other taunt, but he clearly thought better of it, for his lips clamped shut and he merely stared at Rafferty with dislike. At least he no longer leaned back gazing at them with that infuriating condescension. 'So where did you get the funding to get started?'

'That's none of your business.'

This looked like turning into a grudge match. Llewellyn stepped in to referee. 'Mr Blythe, we're here as part of our investigation into the death of a Mr John Harrison who worked as a collector for Malcolm Forbes. He was found dead after being brutally attacked in the alleyway that runs behind one of the rows of houses in Primrose Avenue. You told me on the phone that you saw him enter the alley and took pains that he didn't see you. Did you see anyone or anything else?'

Mollified at Llewellyn's gentler tones, Nigel sat back again. 'No. I saw nothing but what I've already told you. And yes, of course I took pains that he didn't see me. I saw no point in antagonizing him or his boss.' He leaned back in his seat. 'Now, if that's all, I'd like to get on. I do have a business to run.'

'Wanted to avoid another confrontation about whose turf it was? Very wise,' Rafferty put in.

'I've always found that a little discretion goes a long way to reducing any potential hostility.'

'So you didn't follow Harrison into the alley and bop him on the back of the head?'

'Certainly not! I dislike alleys. They're dreadfully muddy places usually and can ruin a decent pair of shoes.'

Llewellyn once again intervened. 'Did you see anything at all, sir?'

'A pretty lady is all. A Ms Tracey Stubbs. One of my clientele. Oh,' he added, 'and a few scruffy brats. There was a gang of youths hanging around the corner, too, when I arrived. I didn't see anyone else. I was more concerned that one of the brats might scratch my car than with doing your job for you.' This last was, of course, directed at Rafferty.

Immediately, he shot back, 'That's a shame because you're

on our suspect list. You were in the right place at the right
time. Maybe you decided to bump off one of your rival's
men.'

'Who do you think I am? Al Capone?' Nigel clearly didn't
deign this worthy of any other reply.

Rafferty didn't really believe that Nigel was the guilty
party anyway. He couldn't see his immaculately-dressed
cousin attacking the large outhouse that was Jaws Harrison.
Certainly not in broad daylight and in a muddy alley.

This interview was turning out to be as much of a waste
of time as his visit to The Elmhurst had been. It made him
short-tempered and he didn't have any hesitation in taking
it out on Nigel.

'Coming the heavy yourself, aren't you, coz?' Nigel
drawled sarcastically. 'Perhaps I should call my solicitor?'

'Perhaps you should, *coz*. If you think you need him.'

Nigel sat up straight and glared at Rafferty. 'I'm beginning to think I might. You come in here, flinging accusations
about and—'

'No accusations, coz. I was merely politely informing you
of your position. No accusation in that.' Rafferty's voice
became sharper. '*Did* you see anything? Anything at all?'

'Only Tracey Stubbs, the kids, the back of Jaws Harrison's
head – not in close-up, whatever you might think – and the
cool dude youths, as I told you.'

'According to our information you were with Ms Stubbs
for some time.'

'She was trying to give me the runaround.'

'So what happened? Did you decide to take payment in
kind? As I said, we heard you were in there some time.'

'My dear Inspector, please. Payment in kind? From little
Tracey? I hardly think so. Of course she might suit *you*. I,
on the other hand, as you know, have more discerning tastes.
I'd only to click my fingers and I could have a dozen Traceys.
If I wanted them. Which I don't. No. From her all I wanted
was what was due and that was money.'

'And did you get it? The money, I mean?'

'Oh, yes. Calm your fears, dear boy. I got my money.'

Rafferty didn't doubt it. Nigel never let more tender feelings come between himself and his first love. 'Don't forget

to let me know if you hear anything,' Rafferty reminded him as he got up.

'Always glad to help the police.'

Yeah, right, thought Rafferty as he walked through the modern chrome and black leather outer office and left Nigel to his empire-building.

By now they were well into the third day of the investigation. The case plodded its slow way on. More people were questioned and their answers checked, but they were no nearer to a solution. The murder weapon still hadn't turned up. Rafferty was beginning to doubt they'd ever find it. There had certainly been no trace of it in Primrose Avenue or anywhere in the immediate vicinity. The search for this elusive item had now spread further afield.

Time, he thought, to question the four youths again. They were the only ones on the spot both before and after the murder. The only ones able if not willing to tell them who else had entered the alley. Who were they protecting? The only thing he could think of was that the youths had some connection to Malcolm Forbes. He seemed just the sort of man who would make use of such youths for his own purposes. Had they seen one of Forbes's other men follow Jaws with intent to extract retribution for some suspected felony? Had Jaws been helping himself to some of Forbes's collection money?

Rafferty didn't know. And the only way they would have any possible hope of finding out was to question the four youths again. They were the only ones – apart from the murderer, unless he was one of them – able to tell them more.

They found them in their usual haunt on the corner of Primrose Avenue. Like Nigel, their memories didn't improve with further questioning.

'Come on, lads,' Rafferty encouraged. 'You must have seen something else.'

'Well, we didn't,' Jake Sterling told him truculently. 'Why do you keep picking on us? We haven't done nothing.'

'So it follows that you must have done something,' Llewellyn said.

'Don't you twist my words.' Jake came forward a few

paces and stood practically nose to nose with Llewellyn. 'I told you we've done nothing. You can believe us or not. My old man knows the law. You can't charge us. You've no evidence.'

Frustrated that they seemed to find murder a subject for aggression rather than horror, Rafferty said, 'Come on, Dafyd. It's clear we're going to get nothing of value from them.'

He turned to the group of youngsters who were hanging around some yards from the youths. One of the kids even sported a leather jacket. Hoping to learn how to be hard and cool, too, thought Rafferty, noting down yet another probable future youth crime statistic.

'Hey, copper,' one of these youngsters, a stocky, ginger-haired lad of about ten, shouted. 'Have you questioned that fatso, Forbes, yet?'

Rafferty wondered whether to grace this mannerless question with a reply, but then he thought, Why not? 'And why would I want to question Mr Forbes? Apart from asking him what he knows about his dead employee?'

'You wanna try asking him how he came to be dead,' the boy scornfully replied. 'Reckon he might know more about it than he's told you.'

'You do, do you? And why might that be?'

'I saw him, didn't I?'

His friends tried to shush him. But it was clear that here was a Malcolm Forbes in miniature, fearless, pugnacious and sure of himself. He was big for his age and his cocky demeanour demanded he show both no fear and a knowledge greater than the rest.

'You saw him, you said? Where was this? And what time?'

His sharp tone did nothing to disconcert the boy. The massed freckles of the true redhead seemed to dance about across his nose and cheeks in his determined effort not to betray his excitement. 'Yeah. I saw him. He came waddling along the street after he got out of that flash Merc he drives. It was around quarter past three. He headed down the alley straight after Jaws had gone down there. When he came out he had something in his hand.'

'What? And where were you that you were able to see him?'

'I was in my bedroom, wasn't I? I live in one of the houses opposite the alley. I was playing a computer game.'

'You didn't say what he had in his hand.'

The freckles seemed to dim with his disappointment as he said, 'That's 'cos I couldn't see it. He had it on the side away from me. Maybe he was hiding whatever it was?' In a fortissimo whisper that betrayed his excitement, he added, 'Maybe he sensed me watching him.'

And maybe you're just making it all up in order to have a bit of fun at my expense, Rafferty thought as he asked, 'Is your mother in?'

'What's that got to do with anything?'

'I don't know yet. Your evidence could be important,' he told the boy, who gave a gap-toothed grin. 'I need to check it out.'

The grin vanished. 'Are you saying I'm a liar?'

'No. Not at all. But it's never wise for a policeman to take everything as gospel. For instance, how do you know Mr Forbes?'

The boy gave as good a sneer as Jake Sterling, he of the cool leather jacket. 'My mum spends enough time in his pawnshop trying to sweet talk old skinny who works there into giving her more money for her stuff. She always drags me and my brother with her. She only got my computer out of hock last week.' He gave a hard-done-by sigh. 'I suppose it'll be going back next week when she can't pay the rent.'

'I see. What number do you live at, sonny?'

'Don't "sonny" me. My name's Bazza. And I live at number thirteen.'

'I'll see what your mum has to say and then I may want to speak to you again.'

Bazza shrugged. 'Suit yourself. But I know what I saw and what time I saw it an' all.'

If the boy's evidence was true it could mean the case made a big push forward. He'd been very definite about the times, too. 'You said you saw the victim, Mr Harrison, a little before Mr Forbes?'

Bazza nodded. 'No more than a minute or so earlier.'

'Did you see him come out of the alley as well?' It didn't seem likely that he had done so, but seeing as he had such a willing witness he might as well check.

'Nah. I only saw him go in. I never saw him come out again, though I waited so I could warn my mum he'd be round. He always does Primrose Avenue before he does our street. I knew she didn't have the money to pay him. She'd been moaning about it earlier.'

'OK, Bazza. You've been very helpful.'

'Think he's telling the truth?' Llewellyn asked as they crossed the road to number thirteen in the street that formed the crossbar of the 'T' with Primrose Avenue.

'God knows. If he copies the example of the big boys in the street, lying will be a way of life. Though why even a kid of his age should be so keen to get on the wrong side of Malcolm Forbes . . . But if his mum confirms he was in his bedroom and that he'd got a good view of the alley, we'll have to take what he says seriously.'

As it turned out, Bazza had told them the truth. Or, at least, he had been in his front-facing bedroom at the time he claimed. His mum, a Ms Lomond, confirmed that her eldest had been in his bedroom from around two thirty to the time the police had turned up when, like the rest of the neighbourhood, he went out to gawp. She was obliging enough to lead them up the stairs to Bazza's bedroom and he did, indeed, have a bird's-eye view of the alley in which the murder had occurred, though high hedging obscured the further reaches of the alley where it curved before meeting the high blank wall of the factory.

It seemed they now, in Malcolm The Enforcer Forbes, had another suspect to add to those in Primrose Avenue. A suspect, moreover, who it seemed certain wouldn't shy away from committing a violent murder if it suited his purposes. And if Jaws *had* been stealing from him, Rafferty could imagine Forbes would consider murder a suitable punishment.

Eight

Another visit to Malcolm Forbes was indicated, but as Bazza's front door shut behind them, Rafferty said, 'I think we'll leave it till tomorrow. If he thinks he's got away with lying to us he might just become over-confident in the interim and let something slip.'

'You know he's likely to deny being in that alley,' Llewellyn put in. 'We've only got young Bazza's word that he was there at all. Even Tony Moran didn't mention his presence.'

'That's why it'll be interesting to see what he says when we question him. Hopefully, his car will show up on CCTV as he passed through the town. In the meantime, we need to see if anyone other than Bazza Lomond saw him. The four youths, for instance. As you say, it's strange that Tony Moran never mentioned him. Though I suppose he was more concerned with saving his skin if he mentioned Forbes than he was with bringing Harrison's killer to justice. Get the house-to-house team on to questioning around the neighbourhood again, will you? Someone else in Bazza's street might have seen him drive up.'

Rafferty, conscious that they might have found the breakthrough that would provide the answers they sought, did his best to quell the burgeoning excitement.

'I hear you're looking for a cheap florist,' Constable Bill Beard said to Rafferty as he and Llewellyn entered the station reception.

'Not a cheap florist, no,' Rafferty corrected him. 'I'm looking for a professional florist who'll do a good job cheaply for my wedding. Why? Know any?'

'My auntie used to be a florist. She's long since retired,

of course. But she likes to keep her hand in. How much were you thinking of paying?'

Rafferty called to mind the quotes he'd had and halved the cheapest.

'I'll give her a bell. You want the usual, I take it? Flowers for the church and reception hall and bouquets and button-holes?'

Rafferty nodded. 'I can let you know how many nearer the time.'

'Numbers aren't a problem. My auntie can always call in the help of a few of her old muckers in the trade. Of course I'll expect an agent's fee.'

'How much?'

'Not the usual fifteen per cent. Not even ten. To you it's five per cent. Can't say fairer than that. Does a lovely job. You'll be pleased with the result. It's in her blood.'

Rafferty couldn't believe that strangling a bunch of inno-cent flowers with wire could be in anyone's blood. 'It's my fiancée who needs to be pleased. One bouquet looks much the same as another to me.'

'Leave it with me. I'll get it sorted for you.' Beard prised his bulk off the reception counter and picked up the phone, looking far more willing and enthusiastic about tackling this little sideline than he ever did about his real job.

Rafferty thanked him and followed Llewellyn upstairs to his office.

Malcolm Forbes said very little at first when they questioned him again at the police station. He waited while Rafferty placed the two tapes in the recorder, sitting silently while Rafferty spoke their names into the tape.

But once Rafferty began questioning him he was quick to deny being in Primrose Avenue at the time Bazza Lomond claimed to have seen him enter the alley.

'What would I need to go there for?' he not unreasonably asked as he leaned back in his chair. He seemed enclosed in an aura of confidence as if he couldn't envisage anyone being foolhardy enough to place him in the vicinity of a murder. And if someone had, his manner implied that someone could easily be persuaded to change their mind. 'I don't do the

collections. That's what I hire staff for. I've got more important things to do with my time.'

'OK, Mr Forbes. So if you weren't in the alley or its
vicinity around the time of Mr Harrison's murder, which
occurred roughly between two thirty and three thirty, where
were you?'

'I was in my office, Inspector. Where I'm normally to be
found on a weekday. And where I should be now if you
hadn't called me into the station to question me on this
trumped-up charge. You can't trust the staff to provide a
decent valuation on people's more valuable little trinkets. I
see to most of that side of things.'

Decent for whom? Rafferty wondered, though he doubted
the 'decent' valuations went to benefit Forbes's customers.
He challenged Forbes's claim. 'You were seen, you know,
going into that alley.'

Forbes's mean grey eyes swivelled between them for a
second before his gaze turned even meaner and he fixed it
intimidatingly on Rafferty. It was clear he wasn't used to
being contradicted. It was also clear that he meant someone
to pay for the necessity of extracting himself from the mire.

'Nonsense,' he barked. 'Seen? How could I have been
seen? I told you. I wasn't there. Seen by whom, anyway?'

Rafferty smiled. 'You know I can't tell you that, sir.' No
chance of that and give him the opportunity to put the frighteners on the bombastic Bazza Lomond. Though Bazza had
been far from discreet in confiding his news and it must have
been overheard by Jake Sterling and his friends. If they
thought there was money in it they might repeat Bazza's
words to Forbes. For all they knew, the four youths were
already in Forbes's pay; certainly, not one of them had
mentioned the loan shark being in the vicinity of the alley
on the afternoon of the murder. 'Which of your staff was on
duty that afternoon?'

'You're surely not going to question my staff?' Forbes put
on a good show of outrage, though, given young Bazza's
evidence, it must have been an act. 'I'm a respectable busi-
nessman. I would have thought my word good enough.'

'In a murder investigation it's of no more value than that
of any other witness. Or suspect,' Rafferty was quick to tell

him. 'We like to be even-handed. And questioning your staff is the general idea. Was it that thin gentleman we saw last time we were at your shop?'

Forbes's heavy face gave a tight nod. It made him look meaner than ever.

The thin gentleman must have been pursuing other business because he had been replaced by a woman today when they had visited the pawnbroker's to pick up Forbes for questioning. Though he doubted the gentleman would be any more use to him than Nigel had been. As soon as Forbes walked free from the interview room, all the staff would doubtless be suitably primed with the right answers as to Forbes's whereabouts at the time of Harrison's death, if they hadn't been already.

Surprisingly, Forbes gave way. 'Very well,' he snapped. 'Question him if you must. But next time you question either myself or any of my staff I must insist on having my solicitor present.'

'That's your prerogative, sir. Now, if I can have the name of the gentleman and his address?'

With a barely concealed ill-grace, Forbes provided the information. 'Though he'll tell you exactly the same as I've told you,' he said.

Rafferty smiled again. 'I'm sure you're right, sir. But it doesn't hurt to be thorough. I'm sure you'd want us to be the same if it was one of your relatives lying on a slab in the mortuary.'

Forbes said nothing more except to bid them a good afternoon.

Once Forbes had left to be ferried back to his shop in a police car, Rafferty said, 'Let's have a scout around the neighbourhood of Forbes's shop. See where Forbes keeps his car and question the people in the neighbouring businesses. They might be more forthcoming about our loan shark's whereabouts than one of his minions.'

Forbes, it turned out, kept his car, a sleek silver Mercedes, in the yard at the back of the shop. High brick walls separated Forbes's yard from those of his next-door neighbours on either side, so unless one of them had seen him driving off in his car, they would have no more than Bazza's word that he had left the shop at all. Unless, that was, Tony Moran decided to expand on his story or the car showed up clearly on CCTV.

However, this time they struck lucky at the first of Forbes's neighbours that they questioned and wouldn't have to rely on either the easily intimidated Moran, who, it seemed, had already lied to them once, or the often grainy CCTV footage. The town's one remaining independent butcher whose shop was next door to Forbes's pawnbroker's had had a delivery expected and had been keeping an eye out. He had seen Forbes drive out of the alley beside the row of shops. The butcher, a Mr Fred Fortescue, a big, burly man who looked as if he was over-fond of his own wares, was adamant about what he'd seen.

'And what time was this, Mr Fortescue?' Rafferty questioned.

'Time? It'd have been gone three o'clock. I'd just served Mrs Palmer – nice sirloin and some of my own sausages – and I was out on the pavement looking for the delivery chap, when I saw Forbes. I don't like the man. Fancies himself. Blamed me when his car had some of the paint scraped off it the other week. I told him. I said, "Maybe if you didn't drive so fast, your car wouldn't get damaged." You could see he didn't like it. But I'm not frightened of him. I'm one for plain speaking. I don't beat around the bush with anyone, me, as I told him.'

'And it was definitely Mr Forbes. You're quite sure?'

'As sure as I'm standing here. Couldn't mistake him. He was only a couple of yards away from me across the pavement. You should have seen the dirty look he gave me since we had words. Thinks he's someone, that man. He's nowt to me. I don't have to kowtow to him and I'm damned if I will,' the forthright northern butcher told him.

'Which way did he drive?'

'He turned right out of the alley. Went past my shop. Heading out to the George Inn for a business meeting, I shouldn't wonder. Got his fingers in a lot of pies, he has. None of them savoury.'

Rafferty gave the butcher a smile of acknowledgement at this witticism. A right turn would certainly have taken him in the direction of the George. It would also have led him to Primrose Avenue. Even if he still denied being there, Forbes had been caught out in a lie, which was interesting in itself.

Rafferty shook Fred Fortescue's hand. 'You'll come down to the station and make a statement?'

'Glad to if it means you get him for something. Time he was put in his place. I hear tell it were one of his collectors that got clobbered. Can't blame people if they take the law into their own hands when they've got nowt and they've got someone like him on their backs. Man's an out-and-out bully. That Forbes is as nasty a bit of work as you'll see in many a long day. Mark my words. I've met a few in me time.'

Fred Fortescue promised to come along to the station to make a statement that evening after he'd shut up his butcher's shop.

Rafferty smiled all the way to their car, which they'd had to park down a side street. 'That's what I call a result,' he said. 'Wonder what Forbes will have to say for himself now?'

'Very little, I imagine. He did say he'd have his solicitor with him next time we question him, remember?'

'Sure sign of guilt when they reach for their brief with so little reason.'

'Or of someone who knows his rights and insists on having them. We may get nothing at all from him.'

'True. But that's two witnesses who say he wasn't in his shop that afternoon.' They had already retrieved the town CCTV footage and now they'd checked out the car that Forbes drove they should get a third witness from that. 'Ring through with the details of Forbes's vehicle, will you, Dafyd, so the team can make a start checking the CCTV evidence? I reckon, with our questioning in the neighbourhood extended, we might unearth one or two more witnesses. It'd be nice to have a quiverful when we tackle Forbes again.'

But although they weren't destined to obtain Rafferty's hoped-for quiverful of witnesses, the two witnesses they had were firm enough in what they said they had seen, particularly Fred Fortescue, who seemed a very strong witness. He thought it was enough to tackle Forbes again, be he with a brief or without.

Rather than behaving with hostility, as Rafferty had

expected, when questioned again Forbes said very little, as Llewellyn had prophesied. Instead, he fielded his brief, who was small but deadly and stonewalled Rafferty at every turn.

The brief, Anthony Frobisher, was well known in the nick. He fronted several of the local criminal fraternity and was generally hated by the police for protecting his clients so efficiently. Today was no different.

Deciding to go on the attack rather than keep to the quiet, polite manner that had availed him nothing, Rafferty said, 'You realize your client is obstructing a police investigation by his denials? We have more than one witness who places him out of his office at the relevant time. More than one witness who places him at the scene.' The last wasn't strictly true – they only had young Bazza Lomond – but Rafferty thought a little exaggeration worth it. 'Yet all you and your client do is deny he was there.'

'That's because he wasn't there, Inspector,' the brief replied coolly. 'As I and Mr Forbes have repeatedly told you.'

Rafferty managed – just – to stop the scowl forming. 'I must warn you and your client that every inch of that alley and every piece of CCTV film between here and there will be thoroughly examined. If Mr Forbes left the office, as I believe, we'll find out and then we'll be back.'

'I'm sure my client will be happy to make himself available.' The brief, sleek, smooth and deadly, added softly, 'As shall I. But my client and I are both busy men, so I suggest you give us more warning than you gave us today if you wish to question him again.'

Rafferty had little choice but to leave it there. He could, he supposed, have arrested Forbes on a charge of obstruction, but as it was likely his brief would have provided his own form of obstruction to any questions, there was little to be gained. They must hope that either the Forensic boys found something in the vicinity of the alley that proved Forbes had been there or that the CCTV came up with irrefutable proof.

However, as it was likely that Forensic would be some time providing any useful leads, Rafferty didn't waste any of it waiting for answers to come to him from that quarter. Other answers were out there, somewhere, and he was determined to find them. To this end, he and Llewellyn set off to question young Bazza again.

The roads were busy. The welcome bright sunshine had brought people out of their homes. Unfortunately, it meant their journey was stop / start nearly all the way. Rafferty restrained his impatience. But eventually they reached Bazza Lomond's home. His mother opened the door and led them upstairs to her son's bedroom.

Bazza was playing some violent game on his computer and showed a marked reluctance to be torn away from it to answer their questions. But eventually his mother persuaded him to abandon the game and help them, although at first he was inclined to be sulky.

'Tell me, Bazza,' Rafferty asked when he had got his attention, his mother making encouraging noises in the background, 'how did Mr Forbes seem when you saw him on the day of the murder?'

'Seem? How do you mean? I don't know how fatso Forbes normally seems, apart from big and aggressive.'

'What I meant was – was he furtive when he came out of the alley? Did he seem nervous? Did you see any blood on him?'

'Blood? No.' This got his interest and although he had turned halfway back to the screen, now he turned back to face them, though he seemed disappointed to have to make this admission. 'He didn't look anything in particular. Just big and red with that "get out of my way" look to him as if he owns the street.'

He certainly owned half of it in Rafferty's estimation, judging from the number of the residents who were in debt to him.

'You said before that he was carrying something when he came out of the alley,' Llewellyn prompted. 'What about when he entered the alley? Was he carrying something then?'

'I dunno. I never noticed.'

'Have you thought any more about what it might have been that he was carrying?' Rafferty put in.

'Yeah. I've thought and thought. But I didn't see what it was. Do you reckon it might have been a knife?' he asked eagerly.

'It wasn't a knife that killed our victim, Bazza,' Rafferty told the boy.

'No?' He seemed disappointed. 'What was it then?'

Rafferty didn't see any reason not to gratify the boy's curiosity seeing as he'd been so helpful and provided them with their first strong lead. 'We believe it was a hammer, son.'

Bazza pulled a face. 'That's what old Lewis said. You know, the old bloke who found the body. Said Jaws's head had been bashed in. I never believed him.'

'Well, it's true, so if you find a hammer anywhere on your travels, don't touch it, but be sure to report it to me.' Gravely, Rafferty took a card out of his pocket and handed it over. 'If you find a hammer or learn anything else, you give me a bell, Bazza. Promise me?'

'Cool.' Enraptured, the boy gazed at the card as at a treasured possession, his desire to return to his computer game at last forgotten.

It was nice, Rafferty thought as they turned away, that there were still kids about who didn't think the police were the enemy.

Rafferty decided to go to see Father Kelly straight after work in order to get the wedding date booked. He found the priest in his study with papers, as usual, strewn over every surface. He had a new housekeeper, another young woman. She had a lush figure and a propensity to low-necked tops. Just the way the old reprobate liked them. He was in a playful mood. From the smell of his breath, he'd had a couple.

'And isn't it the wedding boy himself, young Lochinvar come out of the west,' Father Kelly greeted him as he poured another glass from the bottle of Jameson's whiskey standing at his elbow and took a hefty swig. 'I wondered when you'd come calling. Your ma said you're finally making a start on getting your wedding organized.'

'That's right, Father. Can you book us in for June next year?'

'Sure and you're already booked. Didn't your mammy book it months ago?'

Rafferty stared at him, stupefied. 'How can she have booked it? We've only just decided on the date ourselves.'

'Not a woman to hang about, Kitty Rafferty. She told me you and Abra would be dithering and she was right. Your ma's a sensible woman and knew it was necessary to get it booked as soon as possible. I set aside a twelve o'clock on the second and fourth Saturdays of the month. You can take your pick.'

Rafferty supposed, as he sipped the Jameson's that the ever hospitable priest had poured for him, that he ought to be grateful that his ma, at least, had shown some foresight. No wonder she'd pushed so keenly for June and had rubbished May. No doubt if they'd decided on June and she'd booked July, she'd have found something disparaging to say about that month as well. Oh well. It was done now. 'Hold on a minute, Father, and I'll check with Abra which date she'd prefer.' After a quick chat on his mobile, Abra confirmed they'd go for the second Saturday.

Father Kelly made a note in his diary. He beamed at Rafferty and insisted on pouring him another drink. 'To celebrate your forthcoming nuptials,' he said. 'Never thought I'd live to see the day, not after your last lot.'

Rafferty and Angie, his late first wife, had had a shotgun wedding and the marriage had gone downhill from there. 'It was just a matter of finding the right woman this time,' he said. 'And now I've found her.'

'It's glad for you, I am.' Father Kelly raised his glass. 'Here's to your young lady. May you be blessed with many babies.'

Rafferty wasn't sure the latter part of the toast was one he wanted to drink to, particularly given that Abra's name meant 'Mother of Multitudes', but he didn't say so to Father Kelly who, like the Pope, another bachelor, thought the world should be filled with Catholic babies and lots of them, whatever the penury of the parents.

They clinked glasses and both took more than a sip.

'Your ma booked the church hall while she was at it,' Father Kelly informed him. 'She said you'd want the complete package.' He gazed at Rafferty under his thick eyebrows. 'You did, didn't you?'

Rafferty, stymied by the manager of The Elmhurst Hotel on the reception venue front, gave a weak nod. 'Of course, Father.

Where else would we want to hold the reception?' Especially since The Elmhurst Hotel and the other swanky places Abra had favoured for the reception were all booked up.

He was feeling sorry for himself over his own ineptitude. But it got better as Father Kelly added, 'Of course, Joseph, I insist on letting you and Abra have the use of the hall for free as a wedding present. After all, I baptised you, presided over your first communion and confirmation and those of the rest of your fine brood of siblings, so it's only fitting that I set you off on the next of life's cycles.'

'That's decent of you, Father. Thank you.' It mightn't be the glamorous reception location that Abra had set her heart on. But as he would tell her, it was the act of getting married, of making a commitment to one another in front of witnesses that was the important part, not all the frills and froth that too often surrounded and obscured the main event.

'I'll confirm it in my other diary.' Father Kelly pulled another book, a red one this time, towards him and made the provisional booking firm. That done, he said, 'Now that we're all official, you must get your young fiancée along so I can give her some instruction.'

'I wanted to talk to you about that, Father. Abra's not very religious and—'

'I wouldn't worry about that, my boy.' Father Kelly beamed, showing his yellow, tombstone teeth. 'Such a lack of conviction leaves a vacuum. And doesn't the saying go that nature abhors a vacuum? I'll soon fill her head with the right stuff, don't you worry about that.'

That was precisely what Rafferty had been worrying about. Abra had said she would be willing to get married in St Boniface only if she wasn't forced to listen to a lot of religious mumbo-jumbo before the big day. To have Father Kelly filling her head with the 'right stuff' was unlikely to go down too well. But again, unless they could get a cancellation to get married elsewhere, it was St Boniface or nowhere. Abra would just have to grin and bear the marriage classes and religious mumbo-jumbo she would have to go through. It was that or find another, non-religious venue and possibly put their wedding back a year.

Father Kelly seemed cock-a-hoop, as if, with this wedding,

he felt he'd got Rafferty into his religious clutches once again and knew exactly what he intended to do with him.

It was a pity, Rafferty mused later as he drove carefully home, mindful of the two large whiskeys he'd consumed and wary of the traffic cops, that neither of them had realized just how far ahead it was necessary to book a wedding; then they could have avoided this religious trap. But Ma, as usual, had got her way. Not only the month, but also the location. Moreover, she'd managed to make them grateful while she was doing it.

Abra would have to be told about the marriage classes, of course. But maybe not yet. She'd specified no religious mumbo-jumbo if they were to marry in St Boniface, but surely even she must suspect that the Catholic Church wouldn't marry anyone without religion entering the frame pretty strongly. He'd wait until the wedding arrangements were more settled. She might be in a calmer frame of mind then and more accepting of their necessity. He hoped so, anyway.

'I've designed and printed out those invitations you asked me to do,' Llewellyn said the next morning as soon as Rafferty got in. 'See what you think.'

Llewellyn handed over three separate cards, each with a different design.

Rafferty studied them. Two were delicate in silver and blue. The third was in bold primary colours which straight away attracted Rafferty's eye. But a wedding day was somehow more the bride's day than the groom's, he acknowledged, so he'd leave it to Abra to choose. 'Thanks, Dafyd,' he said as he pocketed the cards. 'I'll let you know which one Abra goes for. You must let me know how much the cards and inkjet cartridges will cost for the full two hundred print run and I'll reimburse you.'

'You'll do nothing of the sort,' Llewellyn told him. 'Think of them as an early wedding present.'

Rafferty was touched. 'Really? That's good of you, Daff. Cheers.' It made him feel bad about not asking Llewellyn to be his best man. Trouble was, he was in a bit of a quandary about it. Should he ask Llewellyn? Part of him wanted to.

After all, not only had he been Llewellyn's best man, but his sergeant had also played matchmaker between himself and Abra and had done a far better job than his ma, for all her efforts, had ever done. He was also likely to make a good job of the best man role, too, being efficient and organized. But there again, he had two brothers and various friends who would all expect to be asked to do the honours. He couldn't make up his mind. Whoever he chose, someone would be offended. Several someones. Now would be the ideal time to ask him, of course, and he felt awkward that he was unable to do so.

Still, he was more than pleased to be able to tick yet another wedding expense off on his mental checklist. He was doing well. Surprisingly well. So far, he'd managed to organize a free hall for the reception – though, admittedly, that was more his ma's doing than his own – bargain-priced bouquets and other flowers as well as a free wedding cake courtesy of Dafyd's mother-in-law. Now he was getting the invitations done for nothing. He just hoped Abra didn't find out what a cut-price wedding she was getting.

It's not that I'm mean, he mentally recorded his defence, just in case. It's just that I don't want us to start married life deeply in debt. And all for the sake of one day, when they hoped to have a lifetime of days together. 'Just one thing, Daff. I'd be obliged if you didn't mention to Abra or anyone else likely to let the cat out of the bag that you're doing the invitations. I don't want any of them getting the idea that I'm a cheapskate.'

Llewellyn's lips turned up a fraction as he said, 'Particularly not Abra.'

'Got it in one.'

'Don't worry. She won't hear about it from me.'

'Good man.'

Nine

The day passed slowly, with little more by way of evidence coming in. The team were still checking the CCTV footage, but had yet to sight Forbes's Mercedes.

Rafferty had been asking around in the station and had found two members of staff with holiday homes abroad. And in pursuit of his quest for a free foreign honeymoon, he button-holed one of them by the simple expedient of hanging around reception until his quarry walked through the doors.

'Tom, my old mate, my old mucker,' Rafferty began. 'Just the man I wanted to see. Let's go up to the canteen and have some tea. My treat.'

Tom Kendall's thick eyebrows rose. 'Your treat? What are you after, Joe?'

'Me? Why would I be after anything?'

Tom just looked at him, but said nothing. They fell into step and soon they were seated on opposite sides of a table in the canteen, tea and sticky buns before them.

'Planning any holidays this year?' Rafferty enquired disingenuously.

'As a matter of fact, I am. Going to my villa in the south of France in August.'

'You've got your own villa? How'd you manage that, then?'

'By staying married to the same woman. There's nothing like divorce for breaking the bank.'

Rafferty nodded at this piece of wisdom. 'Must make you a bob or two in the season.'

Tom shook his head. 'I never let it out. Too much trouble.'

Rafferty's lips pursed at this. 'What? Not even to family and friends?'

'*Especially* not to them. They're the worst of the lot. State they left the place in the first year we had it. I swore I'd never let it out again.'

'Seems a shame, though. Think of the money you're losing.'

'I prefer to think of the hassle I'm saved.'

Rafferty tried another tack. 'What about colleagues? Careful, tidy colleagues?'

Tom laughed. 'You after a free honeymoon, Joe?'

Rafferty denied it. 'I'd be willing to pay to rent it for a couple of weeks.'

Tom shook his head. 'Careful? Tidy? I think you're forgetting that I've seen the state of your desk and tidy it ain't. Sorry, Joe, but no can do. You'll have to find some other mug.'

Rafferty admitted defeat, finished his tea and went back to his office and his murder.

While they waited on further evidence from various strands of the investigation, Dr Sam 'Dilly' Dally had come up trumps. Slow but thorough, he confirmed over the phone that John Harrison had definitely died in the alley. Half a dozen blows had been struck, any one of which could have killed him and caused the brain haemorrhage.

'Someone strong, you reckon, Sam?' Rafferty asked.

'Not necessarily. Just determined. What looks to have been the first blow suggests it was struck by someone shorter than the victim and right-handed, as I said before. I've tried to be more precise on the time of death, but I couldn't reduce it much. Between three and three thirty is the best I can do.'

'That's a help, Sam. Thanks. It agrees with our other evidence.'

They'd had a brief, preliminary talk with all the residents of Primrose Avenue, but with so much to organize at the beginning of another murder investigation, the chats had been too brief for deeper probing. But now, with the different strands of the case begun and with a more definite timescale for the murder, was the time to see if any of the residents had recalled anything relevant. Rafferty got out his list and checked down it. 'For the moment, let's concentrate on those in Primrose

Avenue who owed Malcolm Forbes money. It's possible some of the other residents with easy access to that alley might have different motives for murdering Harrison, but they'll take some digging out. By the way, I meant to ask how you're getting on with decoding Jaws Harrison's notebook?'

'I haven't had a chance to look at it yet. I've been otherwise engaged for the last few evenings on your invitations.'

'Course you have. Sorry.'

'I'll make a start on it this evening.'

'That'll be great, Daff. Thanks.' He reached for his jacket and told Llewellyn, 'We'll do number five first, Mr and Mrs Jones and their lodger, Peter Allbright. Might as well try to get three of the suspects out of the way in one go. Give them a bell, will you, Daff, and make sure they're at home? When you've done that you can ring the rest on the list and tell them we'll be round either today or tomorrow You've got all the telephone numbers?'

Llewellyn nodded. 'I made sure Uniformed asked for them.' He reached in his pocket for his notebook where he would have noted them down in his neat and legible hand and picked up the phone.

Fifteen minutes later, they were on their way.

Mr and Mrs Harry and Margaret Jones and Peter Allbright, their lodger, were all downstairs awaiting their arrival. The living room was plainly but neatly furnished. It was a tidy room with no evidence of lives lived in the form of books or newspapers or DVDs left out. Other than a selection of family photographs there were no pictures on the walls and few ornaments. Malcolm Forbes hadn't supplied them with details of the amounts each of his debtors owed, but Rafferty had set Llewellyn to chasing up this information so they knew that the Joneses owed ten grand between them and Allbright owed four. The only money coming into the house was Incapacity Benefit for Harry Jones and Jobseeker's Allowance for Peter Allbright and Dennis, the eldest son, who'd been at the job centre at the time of the murder. The younger boy, Billy, the only one with a wage packet coming in, had been at work and, like his brother, was out of the running. With all the Eastern European migrant workers coming into the country and working for lower wages than

the indigenous population there were fewer jobs for the un-
skilled nowadays. The three out-of-work males in the
household would be lucky to find any employment locally.
It was hardly surprising they'd taken out loans: Rafferty knew
how low Incapacity Benefit and JSA payments were. They
would meet only a few of the household bills. Robbing Peter
to pay Paul must be a daily juggle. Had they also robbed
John in order to pay the rest?

Margaret Jones was a tall, languid woman in her mid-
forties. She was thin with protuberant blue eyes that suggested
she might have an under-active thyroid. Her eyes were so
bulbous that Rafferty felt an illogical tingle of anxiety lest
they pop out and shoot across the room at him. Harry Jones,
by contrast, was fairly short and, even though he was now
seated, seemed to exude an excess of energy as though to
make up for the lethargy of his wife. It was he who jumped
up with the offer of tea. Clearly the kettle had already boiled
because he was back in a jiffy with a teapot, five mugs and
milk and sugar on a tray.

Peter Allbright, the Joneses' lodger, sat quietly and un-
obtrusively in the farthest corner. He seemed to be hoping
the armchair would swallow him up, so self-effacing did he
seem. He took his mug of tea and sat nursing it in front of
him as if he hoped it would provide some steamy protection. Even though he was a paying lodger with a right to sit
in the living room, he didn't seem comfortable there. As
soon as they'd gone, Rafferty suspected he'd make a bolt for
the stairs and his bedroom. Tall and skinny, he was all bony
angles with short dark hair and glasses. He looked a bit of
a geek with little in the way of social skills and with his
prominently knuckled hands knotted together in his lap.

After taking in this trio of anxious interviewees, Rafferty
said, 'If I can start with you, Mr Jones? I understand you
were working in the back garden around the time of the
attack?'

Harry Jones gave a quicksilver nod. 'Me and Peter. He was
giving me a hand to put up some new fencing between us
and them students. It had been stop and start with the weather
so poor, but I was keen to get it done and we had a fair bit
of protection from the wind from the high factory wall.'

'I see. And you told my officers that you never saw Mr Harrison?'

Briefly, Harry Jones's gaze strayed in Allbright's direction before it turned to meet Rafferty's squarely. 'That's right,' he said firmly. 'Never saw hide nor hair of him, did we, Peter?'

Peter Allbright twisted his hands even more tightly together around his mug and shook his head. So far, he'd not uttered a word. Rafferty was beginning to wonder if he was dumb.

'I had the money all ready for him, ours and Peter's, behind the clock on the mantelpiece in an envelope,' Margaret Jones put in from where she was comfortably cushioned on the beige settee, 'but he didn't knock at the front, either.'

'Wasn't that unusual? I understood Mr Harrison came round for his money every Friday afternoon, even if the times varied.'

'Yes. It was unusual. I can't understand it. I've already told all this to the other officers. Unless he decided to start his collection at the farthest end of the street and was killed before he reached us, though none of the neighbours saw him either. Not according to Emily Parker. I suppose he must have died before he could collect a penny. It's the only explanation, don't you think, Inspector?'

Rafferty didn't think it was the only explanation at all. He sipped his tea, then asked, 'Did you hear any cries? Or anything at all while you were out in the garden?' he asked the two men.

'No,' said Harry Jones, while Allbright just shook his head again. 'But Tracey Stubbs's kids at number nine were in the garden making their usual racket,' Harry went on. 'That family can't do anything without a lot of shouting and hollering. They'd have masked any cries.'

This, Rafferty recalled, was one of the houses that were missing a hammer and Margaret Jones had been one of several women who had left the street on some errand before the murder had been reported. Had the men, one or both, killed Harrison and given her the hammer to dispose of under the pretext of popping to the local parade of shops?

It was certainly a possibility. All three had debts they must have struggled to repay and judging from the scarcity of

ornaments in the living room, little or nothing worth selling
to make the payments. Killing Jaws Harrison and robbing
him of the money in his wallet and the cash in his collection pouch would have tided them over for a bit.

Rafferty had checked out Harrison's collection round with
Malcolm Forbes. He'd have collected a tidy sum by the time
he reached Primrose Avenue. All the debtors on his rounds
were being questioned. He'd considered organizing a recon-
struction of the man's Friday routine, but he had thought it
would reveal nothing further and would cause Superintendent
Bradley to scream blue murder at the costs involved, so had
put it off for future consideration in the event that they failed
to solve the crime in the ensuing few weeks.

He and Llewellyn questioned the three for several more
minutes before Rafferty accepted that none of them was going
to be shifted from the stance they'd adopted. It wasn't a good
start.

'Hope we have better luck with the rest,' Rafferty commented
as the door of number five shut behind them. He heard someone, presumably the shy and retiring Allbright, thumping up
the stairs behind them through the cheap front door. 'Let's
do the pensioner, Mrs Parker, next. Number thirteen. Then
we'll work our way back down the row.'

After a bright start, the day had turned overcast. It was
raining heavily as they left number five and they hurried up
the path and round to Mrs Parker's front door.

Emily Parker looked to be in her late sixties. She was a
plump woman with arms like hams and inquisitive little eyes
that looked as if they'd miss nothing. Unlike Allbright, she
was far from dumb and started chatting away at them before
they'd got over the step. Warned of their visit, she'd taken
the trouble to put on some face powder and lipstick. Even
her hair looked as if it had been specially brushed just so
for the occasion, with hairspray liberally applied. The
perfume coming from it made Rafferty's nose twitch.

Strangely, given the circumstances, she seemed pleased to
see them, for she chattered with barely a pause for breath,
about the murder and poor John Harrison and wasn't it a
wicked shame and so on, ad infinitum. The kitchen was just
off the living room and she continued in this vein all the

while she was making tea and bringing the digestives, even though they'd both said they needed nothing. If it wasn't for his ma's warning that Emily Parker spent most of her time in the neighbours' homes, he would have surmised that she was lonely, but, given her dropping-in propensities, she could have barely given herself the chance to feel such an emotion. Still, she couldn't have had much of an outlet for socializing with her only neighbour, the other pensioner, Jim Jenkins, at number eleven. He'd more or less admitted at their first chat that he did his best to avoid her. Given that she'd barely paused for breath since their arrival, Rafferty could hardly blame Jenkins his avoidance of her. The woman's words came out in such a relentless torrent they were like a physical force one had to fight against. But eventually, Rafferty managed to break the flow to pose a question.

'See Mr Harrison?' she repeated. 'No. I didn't. It's very strange. I've been talking about it to the neighbours and they all think it odd. I've still got my money waiting for him under the clock.' She nodded over to the unattractive Fifties tiled fireplace.

Emily Parker only owed Forbes a thousand pounds, though presumably, as she was a pensioner, it was enough. According to Forbes's accounts, she was paying the debt off regularly, though there had been several weeks in the last few months when she had failed to make a payment. She must find it a struggle, as she admitted she only had her pension. But, like Jim Jenkins, she was of the generation who believed in paying their dues. Though, to judge from the lack of knick-knacks, she had perhaps been selling her treasures in order to make the repayments.

'Tell me, Mrs Parker, why did you take out a loan?' Rafferty asked. He thought he might as well get the background.

She sighed. 'It's the grandchildren, Inspector. I've six of them and it's so difficult to manage to afford to buy them something nice for their birthdays and for Christmas. It was the eldest's eighteenth birthday in December. Two of them were born then and another at the beginning of January. All clumped together around Christmas with all its extra expense. Of course I had to get him something nice for such a special birthday. I didn't have the money, even though I try to put something by out of my pension each month. It was such a worry.'

'You could have applied for a credit card, Mrs Parker,' Llewellyn put in. 'The interest would have been less onerous than that which Mr Forbes charges.'

She nodded. 'I know that. But I was reluctant to apply for one. Tracey Stubbs at number nine has several and she has a terrible time juggling the payments. I was worried that once I had one I might keep using it. I didn't want the temptation. At least by taking a loan out with Mr Forbes, I don't have a card always there and handy.'

Rafferty could see her point. It was the same reason his ma gave for not using credit cards. It was a good argument – until, as Llewellyn had pointed out, you looked at the interest rates and the potential threat of violence from the alternatives. At least the credit card companies stopped short of sending the boys round, though, he supposed, they'd do that as well eventually, if they had to have debts chased by debt collectors.

'Why don't you explain your financial position to your family?' Llewellyn asked gently. 'I'm sure they wouldn't expect expensive gifts if they realized your situation.'

'Oh, no! I couldn't do that. I don't like to worry them. And they have their own troubles without loading mine on to their shoulders, too.'

It was pride, Rafferty assumed. A lot of people didn't like to admit they couldn't afford to buy the youngsters in the family the expensive trainers and other designer gear they clamoured for. Let the little buggers get Saturday jobs and pay for them themselves if they were such must-haves. When his nieces and nephews were younger, his ma would organize all the present-buying for him. But generally nowadays, he just put a tenner in the card and left it at that; his ignorance about teen fashion matched his reluctance to pay for it. But he supposed he was lucky, as men were seldom expected to make much effort in the gift department.

But, he reminded himself, they weren't here as social workers. They were here to try to solve a murder and now he reapplied himself to the purpose of their visit. Like the Joneses and Peter Allbright, Emily Parker claimed not to have set eyes or ears on Harrison on Friday. Not one of the residents had so far admitted to seeing him or to hearing any cries other than those from Tracey Stubbs's children. He was beginning to believe they had all got together to agree their stories in the time between Eric Lewis finding the body and his dialling 999 at five o'clock. He could understand why the murderer would be happy to collude in such a plan, but not why the rest might have gone along with it. Unless they were all – bar one, the murderer – telling the truth and Harrison *had* been killed before he'd had a chance to collect any of the money owed.

They received the same answers from the soon-to-be married Josie McBride at number three and the Smiths' 'ology' student lodger, Samantha Dicker at number one.

Both young women were in Josie's home when they went to question her, which was convenient.

In spite of the recent too-close murder, the two girls seemed far away from doom and death and had clearly been deeply immersed in holiday brochures filled, as were Rafferty's, with exotic holiday destinations. The brochures were spread all over the floor, on the table and chairs. With a little moue of annoyance at having her wedding planning interrupted, Josie McBride cleared some of the clutter away so they could sit down.

'Ms McBride, Ms Dicker,' Rafferty began. 'As you probably know, we've been questioning the other residents and—'

'Yes,' Josie McBride broke in. 'We wondered when you'd get around to us. Not that we can tell you anything.'

The fair-haired Samantha Dicker put in, 'I was studying all afternoon and didn't notice a thing.'

'And what about you, Ms McBride?' Rafferty asked. 'What were you doing?'

She laughed and tossed back her thick dark hair. 'Probably what I spend most of my spare time doing – planning my wedding.'

My wedding, she'd called it. Briefly, Rafferty wondered if that was how Abra thought of their big day. As *her* wedding, rather than theirs. It might explain a lot.

'You were both alone, I take it?'

The two girls looked at one another and nodded. 'My fiancé was around my mother's house doing some DIY for her,' Josie explained. 'But I already told the other officers that.'

'I'm afraid something as serious as a murder inquiry brings a lot of repetitive questions.'

'Hoping to catch us out?' the vivacious Josie put in.

'Only if there's anything you can be caught out about,' Llewellyn quietly reminded her.

'Well, there's not. And neither is there for Sam. Neither of us saw or heard a thing. It's not as if he died down our end of the alley, so we wouldn't have been likely to hear anything. I doubt if I would anyway, as I had some music on while I was finishing the wedding present list.'

Rafferty nodded. 'So, when's the happy day?'

'Not till September next year. But you've got to get organized early these days if you want your first choice of venue, photographer and the rest.'

As Rafferty had learned to his cost. He'd been a little too relaxed about the whole thing. But so many weddings nowadays were such crazed and costly affairs. So different from his first wedding, which had, of course, because of Angie's pregnancy been quickly arranged and done relatively cheaply. It hadn't cost much more than a thousand pounds – even Angie's dress had been a second-hand and never-before-worn outfit from an ad in the local paper. But at the time he'd thought it all costly enough. They'd had the reception in one of the local pubs with a wannabe DJ friend spinning the discs.

He hadn't told any of this to Abra. He'd implied that he'd let Angie have her way on everything, mainly because he didn't want Abra to think he'd been a cheapskate twice over. But it was true that he'd begrudged every penny he'd been forced to spend on that wedding because he hadn't wanted to get married. Talk about being careful about where you planted your seed.

He came to from his reverie to find Josie McBride, Samantha Dicker and Llewellyn staring at him expectantly. He rose from his chair. 'We'll be off,' he said. 'If you remember anything. Anything at all—'

'We know. Contact you,' Josie said pertly. 'But as there's nothing for us to remember.'

Rafferty mused about the two young women after they took their leave of them.

Samantha Dicker was the quieter of the two, every inch the 'ology' student, from her owl-like glasses to her dowdy, calf-length brown skirt.

Both girls were in debt. Josie McBride had taken a loan out from Malcolm Forbes to pay part of her wedding costs and Samantha Dicker had taken one out when she'd exceeded her student loan limit. It seemed likely that both might be having trouble meeting the repayments. The two seemed very close, the one so dark and the other so fair and both so deeply in debt.

Had they colluded in killing Harrison? There again, both seemed bright girls and must surely have realized that killing Harrison would only put off their repayment problems by a matter of days while Forbes rearranged his collection routes or took on and trained a replacement collector.

Still, Josie's shed was missing its hammer, as was the Smiths' where Samantha lodged. Josie had also been one of the three women who had left the street after the murder and before Uniformed's arrival and so could have disposed of the murder weapon.

But, Rafferty reflected as he and Llewellyn shut the gate and crossed the street, all the maybes and ifs were only that. Many maybes and ifs clung to the other residents too, several of whom were far more likely to resort to violence than these two. Like Leslie Sterling, for instance, the 'waster' father of Jake and Jason.

Ten

S terling's wife was at work when they called, as she had been on the day of the murder. They found Les Sterling in his vest with the racing blaring out on the television. There was no sign of his two sons.

The house, as they walked through from the hall, had an uncared-for air. Even Rafferty, not usually one to notice such things, couldn't help but see the dust thick on the skirting boards and the plentiful spiders' webs draped from the ceiling corners. Clean clothes were piled in heaps on the arm and back of the worn settee waiting for someone, presumably Mrs Sterling, the only working member of the family, to take them upstairs and put them away.

Sterling had a stack of betting slips and several empty lager cans on the table beside his chair, into which he slumped immediately after letting them in. He looked set for the day. Perhaps he spent every day like that. He was inclined to be surly, a surliness doubtless fuelled by the alcohol he had already consumed. After meeting his two sons, Rafferty had half-expected a less than gracious welcome. The apples certainly hadn't fallen far from the tree in his case. Sterling owed Forbes six thousand pounds. It looked like he was trying to solve his problems by gambling his way through them. But, to judge from the number of torn-up betting slips littering the floor, his plan was going awry.

'It's never a good idea to look to the bookies to solve your money problems, Mr Sterling,' Rafferty pointed out. He got no thanks for this piece of gratuitous advice, however.

'What's it got to do with you?' Sterling rubbed pork sausage fingers through his thinning reddish-blond locks and glared at him from bloodshot brown eyes. He took a swig from the open lager can and then demanded belligerently, 'And why aren't you interviewing anyone else but me on this side of the street? I saw you across the road. You made a beeline for my place after questioning the lot across the way.'

The Sterlings lived at number ten – not, as he said, on the side of the street that backed on to the alley where Harrison's body had been found. It was clear he felt he was being picked on. But given his family's history he could scarcely be surprised at that.

'Your neighbours in this row have already been questioned once, Mr Sterling, and will be so again.' He didn't add that Sterling was the only resident on this side of the street to owe Forbes money.

'But you decided to do me first the second time around, is that it?'

That was exactly it, but Rafferty felt exonerated from the accusation that he was picking on Sterling Senior in view of the fact that not only was he yet another of Forbes's debtors, but he had also had two of his sons hanging round at the top of the street, either of whom could have tipped him the wink on Harrison's arrival. The day of the murder had been wet, chilly and blustery; not one in which anyone would choose to go out if they didn't have to. Les Sterling could have slipped out of his back door and up the right-hand-side alley with a good chance, for a betting man, that none of his neighbours would see him. Of course, any of his neighbours could also have slipped out. But none of them had two sons keeping cavie on the corner.

Sterling, as expected, denied leaving the house.

'Killing someone? Not me. And certainly not that bastard Malcolm Forbes's man. Kick your head in soon as look at you that lot. If I was worried about not being able to pay my bills I'd go for the head honcho, not his lackeys. I'd petrol bomb the bastard where he keeps his records. What would be the point of going for one of the lackeys? It would be stupid. And I'm not stupid.'

No, thought Rafferty. You're just a bone idle sponger. But Sterling had made the same point he had himself hit on early in the case. And he was right. Petrol bombs would have settled the debt problem nicely. With the records destroyed who was to say who were the debtors?

Having learned little more than the unpleasing thought that Sterling was on a similar wavelength to himself, Rafferty, as they returned to the station to write up their reports, admitted that they knew little more than they had known before. Even their reports would be the same as those they had made the first time round, which wouldn't please Superintendent Bradley.

Bill Beard hailed him as he came into reception. 'I've had a word with my auntie and she said she'll be glad to help you out with your wedding flowers She said she'd have done it cheaper than the price you named if only because of all the laughs she's had at your expense over the years. But as I told her, a deal's a deal.'

You've done yourself, Rafferty told the groom. But even though he now found Bill's aunt would have done the flowers for an even lower price than the one he'd suggested, he was chuffed. 'That's great, Bill. Give me her number and I'll get Abra to get on to her with her exact requirements.'

Bill reached for a blank witness statement form and scribbled a number down. 'She lives here in Elmhurst so she's nice and handy.'

'Thanks, Bill. I owe you one.' He was owing a lot all ways round.

'That's right. I might call in the favour one of these days. Don't forget I shall expect an invite to the wedding.'

'And you shall get one. You and auntie both.'

Once they had finished writing the latest reports on the case, Rafferty threw the last one down on the pile. 'I'm done in,' he said. He glanced at the clock and smiled. 'Nice timing. A spot of lunch is called for. Fancy a bite at the Black Swan?' he asked Llewellyn.

Llewellyn nodded. 'Just half an hour, though. Remember, we've more interviews this afternoon.'

Rafferty pulled a face at this reminder. 'Don't be a spoilsport, Daff. What is it they say about all work and no play?'

'Point taken. But what if Superintendent Bradley wants to see you for an update and you go to his office smelling of beer?'

'I'll smell as much from half a pint as I will from two. Anyway, that's what breath fresheners are for.' Rafferty sighed. 'Come on. We're five minutes into our precious half-hour already. If we investigate any more things that *might* happen this afternoon – like Bradley wanting an update – it'll be time to come back before we've gone.'

To forestall any other reasons for not going to the pub, Rafferty put on his jacket and made for the door. As they reached the car, he tossed the keys to Llewellyn. 'You drive,' he said. 'I want to do some thinking on the way. Let no one say I don't use my leisure time productively.'

'You can't drive *and* think?'

'Not according to Abra. She says men can't multitask. At least that's what she says when I'm driving and trying to read road signs at the same time.'

It didn't take more than a few minutes to reach the pub. Situated on the river like several others in Elmhurst, the Black Swan was an old pub, filled with low beams dark with age and smoke. They had beaten the lunchtime crowd and were quickly served, Rafferty with a pint of Adnams bitter and Llewellyn mineral water. After placing their food order, they went into the garden. They had only been sitting for five minutes when their order of a Ploughman's each arrived.

They ate in silence for a few minutes enjoying the crusty French bread and the sharp taste of a mature cheddar, its sharpness heightened by the tang of pickles.

It was a pleasant day after all the recent rain and the pub garden was bathed in sunshine. It was quiet and the sound of birdsong came to them clearly above the gentle gurgle of the river. The Black Swan's garden was a veritable paradise on such a day. A warm breeze caressed them and Rafferty took off his jacket and stretched. 'Sure we can spare only half an hour?' he asked. 'Me, I could spend the rest of the day here, just idling –' he grinned – 'and thinking through our current investigation, of course. I can do it just as well here as at the office.' And without the danger of Superintendent Bradley interrupting their quiet idyll.

But Llewellyn had other ideas. 'There's been extensive local media coverage on this case,' he reminded Rafferty. 'It wouldn't do if one of the local press had followed us here and reported that we idled the afternoon away instead of being seen to get on with the investigation. If it got back to the superintendent—'

'All right, all right, I get the drift. I hardly need Long Pockets Bradley on my case when I've got you, do I?' He took a long pull from his beer and even though the minutes of their short half-hour were ticking away, he sighed contentedly. It was only as his mind dwelled on the wedding and the still spiralling cost of the parts of it that Abra had charge of that some of his contentment seeped away. He asked Llewellyn, 'How did you keep the costs down on your wedding? Ours are getting beyond a joke, even with you doing the invitations and Bill Beard's auntie doing the flowers. Abra seems to have developed a Princess Di complex. I can't seem to rein her in.'

'I was lucky, I suppose, in that Maureen isn't given to ostentation or extravagance. I'm an only child, too, which reduced the guest list. I suppose we just worked on it together.'

'What? No arguments? I keep getting the "aren't I worth it?" line from Abra. What am I supposed to say to that?'

'That's a tricky one. Can't you reason with her?'

'She's beyond reason most of the time. The things she thinks are essential are ridiculous to my mind. She wants me and the other men in morning suits, if you please. She wants a rehearsal dinner, a five-tier wedding cake. She wants a theme to the wedding – her current fancy is for an oriental do. She even wants wedding favours, whatever they are. I didn't dare ask.'

'I believe they're gifts for the guests. Little mementoes of the day.'

'Gifts for the guests? I thought it was them who are meant to buy us presents, not the other way round!'

Llewellyn smiled as he finished his meal. 'You don't need to buy anything extravagant, though something more expensive is appropriate for the bridesmaids and the best man.'

Was that a hint? Rafferty wondered. That was yet another problem; he hadn't yet decided who to ask to undertake the role. There were several candidates, including Llewellyn.

'As I said, we kept a lid on things for our wedding, though

we did have favours for the bridesmaids – a locket and chain each. I have to admit, though, that I've heard Abra discussing the wedding with Maureen and she'd frighten me with her plans. What are you going to do?'

'God knows. I'm at my wits' end with it all. I don't know why we have to have all this fuss.'

'I hope you're not going off the idea of getting married?'

'Of course not.' Abra was Llewellyn's cousin, so he was naturally concerned. But the relationship constrained Rafferty's desire to have a real heart-to-heart. 'Get Mo to have another word with her, will you, Daff? I just want her to curtail her more fanciful desires and get real before we blow any pretence of having a budget and end up in debt for the next ten years.'

'I'll ask her. Though don't get your hopes up. As you say, Abra's got the bit between her teeth and she's going to take some prising away.'

Rafferty nodded glumly. He was seeing a side to Abra that he hadn't seen before. A side he'd never suspected was there. God knew what she might be committing them to when he wasn't there.

Superintendent Bradley caught him as he came back from the pub – he hadn't even had a chance to use his breath freshener. But fortunately, the super was more intent on having a go at him about his current investigations than he was about drinking at lunchtime.

'So if you're getting nowhere on the murder at least tell me you're having more success on the muggings investigation.'

Bradley had his intransigent Yorkshire face on. It told Rafferty he'd have to box clever.

'Funny you should mention the two investigations in the same breath. It's a good point.' It was always wise policy to flatter the super. Give him the sugar first and the nasty medicine went down easier. At least, that was the theory. 'The thing is, I'm not altogether certain the two cases aren't connected. I've got various feelers out on the usual suspects and we've got a prize pair in the Sterling brothers, Jake and Jason. They've both got convictions for violence. These muggings sound right up their street, particularly if they were put up to them by Malcolm Forbes in order to warn off the competition.'

'Forbes? What's he got to do with it? The murder was of one of his own men. You think there might have been a bit of tit for tat amongst the local loan sharks and one of them went in for a bit too much tit with Harrison?'

'Yes, sir. I think you might well be right.' Agreeing with the boss was also a good tactic. 'I wondered whether Forbes might have organized the first two muggings of his competitors when one of them went a whole lot further with Harrison.'

'Mmm. I hope you're right, Rafferty. Go with that theory and bring me some culprits.'

Rafferty nodded and eased himself from the room. That had gone well. Better than he'd hoped. He'd better score some arrests soon, though, on the muggings at least if he was to keep the super sweet.

Rafferty said as soon as he got back to his office, 'Let's have Tony Moran in again. Maybe he can tell us why he made no mention as to Malcolm Forbes's arrival at Primrose Avenue. Moran's been pretty cooperative so far. Perhaps we can get more out of him. We can ask him if he saw Leslie Sterling prowling around the back alley while we're at it.'

But it seemed that either Jake Sterling or one of Forbes's goons had had something of a heart-to-heart with Tony, because he refused to say anything more. This mightn't be unconnected to the fact he looked like he'd sustained something of a beating in the interim. He had two black eyes and had lost one of his front teeth and generally gave off the aura of being sorry he'd opened his mouth at all.

Rafferty sat back and stared at the youth. 'You've been got at, Tony, that's clear. The question is: who got at you? Your tough little friends or Forbes's minions?'

The latter seemed most likely as the CCTV footage had clearly shown Forbes's Mercedes on the road on Friday afternoon. He denied he'd been driving it, but it was a nice car, expensive, so Rafferty doubted Forbes had let anyone else behind the wheel.

'I've got nothing more to say,' Moran mumbled with difficulty through his swollen jaw.

Rafferty couldn't blame him for making the sensible choice. He'd probably do the same in a similar position. If he had got beaten up for telling them the little he had so far shared, even without revealing Forbes's presence in the alley on the day of the murder, what punishment was he likely to receive if he opened his mouth further? Forbes wouldn't be likely to let a potential witness to murder remain above ground.

Although he was sure that Tony Moran could provide back-up to what Bazza Lomond had told them, it was clear the youth had been frightened into silence. They would get nothing incriminating out of him so there was no point in questioning him further. But that didn't apply to Malcolm Forbes. The CCTV footage showed his car and its registration number clearly. If he hadn't been driving it – which, in view of young Bazza's story, seemed unlikely – he must have handed his keys to someone else.

'Give Forbes a bell, Dafyd. I suppose we ought to give him a chance to get his brief organized if we're to get a word out of him. I don't want him doing a "no comment" routine like we had with the two Sterlings and Des Arnott.'

It was a full hour later before Forbes showed up at the station, having, as expected, demanded time to summon his brief.

Although clearly far from pleased at being questioned again, Forbes had made no bones about the appointment. Rather, his voice on the phone had sounded bored as if he found little point in being questioned over trivia such as murder. But that might be because he'd already obtained Moran's silence and felt able to discount Bazza's evidence. The team questioning around the neighbourhood had discovered that young Bazza had earned a reputation as a teller of tall tales. It was likely that Forbes, if he knew of Bazza's involvement, would have already put out feelers on the lad, so he would be aware that his evidence wasn't necessarily as strong as Rafferty had thought.

Rafferty didn't beat about the bush once he and Llewellyn were again seated in the interview room with the man himself and his brief. He simply placed a still photograph from one of the CCTV tapes on the desk squarely under Forbes's nose and said, 'Your car, I believe, Mr Forbes. You can see the time and date of the shot clearly.'

Forbes simply looked at the picture but said nothing for several moments. Then he pointed out, 'That's from the High Street. It doesn't prove my car – or me – was in Primrose Avenue when Harrison was killed.'

'True. But what it does prove, Mr Forbes, is that you lied to me. So, if you weren't heading for Primrose Avenue, where were you going?'

Unexpectedly, Forbes capitulated. Instead of claiming that one of his staff had borrowed his car as Rafferty had expected, he admitted it had been him driving the Merc. 'And you're right, I did go to Primrose Avenue. But I didn't go there to kill Harrison. What reason would I have to do that? I'd gone to get his payment record sheets for last month. The accountant's been asking for them as he wants to get the year's accounts ready for the taxman and I'd forgotten to get them off Harrison earlier.'

It seemed unlikely to Rafferty that Forbes would act as his own messenger boy and he asked, 'Why didn't you send one of your staff? Or ring Harrison himself and get him to drop the sheets off?'

'My staff were all busy and I couldn't get Harrison on his mobile. He must have switched it off. There was nothing much happening in the office so I took a drive out there to collect the sheets myself. I knew roughly where he was likely to be. I knew I was right when I saw his car parked round the corner from Primrose Avenue.'

'And did you get the records?'

'Oh yes. And before you ask, I dropped them off at my accountant's. You can ask him yourself if you don't believe me.'

'I will, Mr Forbes.' Llewellyn jotted down the accountant's details. Rafferty had wondered why a mugger or murderer would trouble to take the payments book in which Harrison would have noted the monies he'd collected. Of course, if the murderer was one of the debtors having trouble with his repayments, he might have taken the book to conceal the fact. But now they knew that hadn't happened and soon he would know if Harrison *had* visited any of the houses in the avenue that afternoon, for surely the payments book would

contain evidence of instalments made against the loans, and
if so, he would be able to confront all those who had claimed
not to have seen him.

'By the way, Mr Forbes, while you're here, I wonder if
you could supply me with a list of *all* your debtors.' It had
occurred to Rafferty earlier that their killer might have
murdered Harrison on someone else's behalf rather than their
own; someone whom Harrison had threatened with violence
for non-payment. It was another possibility that he needed
to investigate.

Rather to Rafferty's surprise, Forbes made no objection.
He held up his mobile and got a nod of acquiescence for its
use from Rafferty and relayed the message to his office staff.
'They'll be waiting for you at the shop.'

'Do you know if any of these people are related to any of
the residents on Primrose Avenue?' he asked.

'No idea.' As Forbes sat back at his ease on the hard plastic
interview room chair, it was clear that he was prepared to
help them so far and no further. 'I don't ask for a list of
their friends and relations when people sign up for loans. I
mostly supply a service to those unable to get credit elsewhere. Those with CCJs against them and other problems.
The loans aren't guaranteed by parents or other relatives.
But I'm a trusting man and when people take out a loan with
me I like to believe they'll repay it.'

With his trust backed up by the collectors, who could turn
menacing at the drop of an excuse. But at least now they had
some of the truth from Forbes. Time would tell if he'd told
them the whole truth. Meanwhile, they would pay a visit to
the accountant and check the payments for Friday. Then they
could check out the names on the latest list of debtors that
Forbes had agreed to supply and which Rafferty assigned
Uniform to collect straight away.

But once Forbes and his brief had left and before they
could do anything else, news came over the squawk box that
another loan shark's collector had been attacked and was
lying badly injured in Elmhurst General.

Eleven

The injured man, a broken-nosed bruiser by the name of Izzy or Ignatius Barber, was at first reluctant to tell them anything, even his name. Though as the nursing staff of Elmhurst General had gone through his pockets after his admission and found a letter with his name and address on, he was forced to acknowledge his identity. But he wasn't in a fit state to withstand their questioning and it wasn't long before he admitted to working for Nigel Blythe. And not long after that he told them he had been on his usual collecting round when he'd been attacked. He seemed even more bruised by the fact that someone had had him over than he did by his bodily injuries. But eventually they drew the rest of the story out of him.

'They took me by surprise, didn't they? Otherwise I wouldn't be lying here now, I can tell you. Bundled me into an alley out by Boadicea Drive. Four of them there were, wearing ski masks. Came up on me from behind. Didn't hear a thing. They beat the shit out of me before they took my wallet and the money I'd collected.'

'Have you any idea who they were, Mr Barber?' Llewellyn asked.

'No. None. Could have been any of the scrotes that live on the manor.'

'I know you didn't see their faces because of the masks they wore, but you must have seen their clothing and footwear. Do you remember anything about that?' Rafferty asked.

'Yeah, now you mention it. Three of them had short leather jackets and all four of them wore trainers. Nikes. Not that that's likely to lead you to them. All the little scrotes wear trainers these days. Just as well for me. If they'd worn heavy boots to give me a kicking I might not be here now.'

It was interesting that Izzy Barber had been attacked no more than a couple of streets away from where John Harrison had died. Was it possible their murder was simply a case of muggers going too far and not a premeditated crime at all? If so, given that Izzy Barber had mentioned that four men had attacked him, the possibility that it had been Jake Sterling and his merry band who had committed the assault occurred to Rafferty. They'd certainly been on the spot when Harrison had been attacked and three of them invariably sported their trademark bum-freezer leather jackets. Maybe they didn't spend all their time hanging around the end of Primrose Avenue waiting for something to happen, but went and got the action going themselves.

Izzy Barber had been able to furnish little else in the way of descriptions of the four males who had attacked him as they had approached from behind. But he said he had managed to get one or two of his flailing fists to connect with faces, so if Jake Sterling's little gang *were* guilty of the latest attack at least one of them would have the bruises to show for it.

Rafferty, not forgetting the possibility that Barber had been attacked as part of a turf war between the local loan sharks, put the possibility to him.

His eyes immediately looked shifty and he denied it. 'Nothing like that. All the local moneylenders get along just fine.'

'Just one big happy family, hmm?' Rafferty queried cynically.

Barber tried a grin but when it proved too painful he abandoned the attempt. 'Yeah,' he agreed.

'And what family would that be? The mafia?'

'No. Of course not. We don't kill one another.'

'Somebody killed Jaws Harrison.'

'That? Just a mugging that went wrong. Nothing else.'

Barber pretended to doze after that. He even started snoring to add verisimilitude.

They left Barber to nurse his bruises and his damaged dignity. Rafferty said as they left the Accident and Emergency Department, 'Let's get over to Forbes's accountant and have a decko at Harrison's payments records. We might be able to shed some light on whether he visited one or more of the avenue's residents before he got topped. Then I think we should see Nigel Blythe again, seeing as it was one of his collectors who just got mugged. If he's got involved in a turf war with Forbes or one of the other loan sharks I want to know about it.

'And when we've done that,' he added as they got in the car, 'you can get the team started on checking out the entire list of Forbes's debtors. It should have been collected by now and be at the station. Maybe we'll unearth one or two of Forbes's other debtors with family related to our investigation. We might unearth a kissing cousin or two who turned into a killing cousin.'

Adrian Stoner, Forbes's accountant, was a slim, sharp-eyed man in his early thirties. At first, he was brusque and unhelpful. He insisted on checking with Forbes before he handed over Jaws Harrison's payments records, but once Forbes had given his OK, he made no further demur.

A quick glance at the payments records told them that the only debtors who hadn't lied to them about not seeing Harrison on the afternoon of his murder were Emily Parker and Les Sterling. A check through the previous pages showed them that Jaws had visited neither as a non-payment was entered as such in his records. There was no such entry against either name.

It made sense. Jaws Harrison had got as far as Emily Parker's back gate before he was attacked.

Having got the accountant to photocopy the relevant records pages and satisfied that they now had some facts to match against the lies they'd been told, Rafferty was keen to tackle Mr and Mrs Jones and their lodger as well as Josie McBride and Samantha Dicker, who had all claimed not to have seen Harrison. And as for Peter Allbright, no wonder the introverted lodger had been so keen to bury himself in his bedroom and away from their questioning. Presumably, he wasn't a very good liar and had sought refuge in silent nods and shakes of the head to indicate affirmative or negative responses.

They would interview all five again tomorrow. Rafferty

didn't particularly look forward to hounding them. But one or more, in collusion, might well have viciously killed a man and he couldn't afford to let the soft sentiment of fellow feeling with other debtors get in the way of his job. Especially when, by their own too ready lies, they'd levered themselves further up the suspect list.

Rafferty would have been glad to call it a night and get home if he didn't know that he faced more indebtedness of his own over his and Abra's wedding plans.

It was at times like this that he felt like chucking in the towel as a copper. Who was it who said that money was the root of all evil? He couldn't remember, but Llewellyn would. He would doubtless also tell him that, as usual, he'd got the quotation wrong.

They went to see Nigel Blythe again after speaking to Izzy Barber and Malcolm Forbes's accountant. Nigel's mood turned truculent after they told him of the attack on his collector.

'This attack on my man is down to Forbes. I know it is.'

'How do you know that?' Rafferty demanded. 'Do you have proof?'

'No, of course I don't have proof. Don't be more stupid than you can help. You know as well as I do that you don't get proof where Forbes is concerned. He makes sure that if there is any that it goes away. But I just know in my guts. His men have been intimidating mine for several weeks, though they won't tell you that.'

'Deal with it themselves, will they? Is that what you're telling me?'

'I'm telling you nothing. I can't tell you what they mean to do. You'll need to speak to them.'

'I intend to. I'll want a list of their details.'

Sulkily, Nigel supplied it.

'I'll also want a list of your debtors. Just in case one of them hit on Izzy Barber.'

Surprisingly, Nigel made no objection to this. In fact, he seemed rather amused as if he knew something Rafferty didn't.

Rafferty discovered what that something was when he had

got back in the car and scanned the list. There, large as life, was the name Mrs Kitty Rafferty. What was she doing borrowing money from slimy Nigel?

'Sure and I needed it for your wedding present, didn't I?' his ma told him after he had gone to her home directly from Nigel's office, leaving Llewellyn to wait in the car. 'There was a special offer and I needed to buy it before they sold out.'

Rafferty would rather not know about Ma's 'special offers'. They were usually the sort that had sneaked out of the back of a lorry in the dark of night.

'You didn't need to borrow money for that, Ma. You only needed to buy us a token present.'

'And me the mother of the groom? What would people say if I bought you a set of cheap saucepans as a wedding gift?'

'Who cares what they'd say? Besides, we've already got a perfectly good set of saucepans. In fact, we've got an entire flatful of stuff. We don't need anything.'

'That's not what Abra says. She's got a list as long as your arm.' This was news to Rafferty. But then, nowadays, most things to do with the wedding seemed to be that. 'Besides, *I* needed to buy something decent. Something that would take pride of place in the gift display at the wedding breakfast.'

'How much did you borrow, Ma?'

'It's not telling you, I am.' His ma's lips firmed stubbornly.

'Come on, Ma. How much? I can always ask Nigel, you know.'

Reluctantly, Ma admitted she'd borrowed £500. 'It was only keeping it in the family, I was.'

'Better than going to Malcolm Forbes, I suppose, but still unnecessary. It's you that Abra and I want at our wedding, not some fancy, overpriced present that puts you in hock.'

Ma looked pleased at this, although still a bit shamefaced that she'd been found out in her borrowing. She was still subdued as Rafferty left, which was something he hadn't seen in many a long year.

*   *   *

Rafferty marched into Nigel's office and slapped a cheque down on his desk. 'I think you'll find that covers Ma's debt.'

'I'd prefer cash.'

'I bet you would.'

'There's an extra charge for early settlement,' Nigel told him, seemingly determined to get the upper hand somehow.

'How much?'

'Fifty should cover it. Seeing as you and Mrs R are family.'

'Don't be doing us any favours, Nigel.'

'OK. Make it a round hundred.'

Bank account unnecessarily dented further by his own intransigence, Rafferty pulled his cheque book out and wrote another cheque, which he ripped out of the book and laid beside the first one. 'And don't lend money to Ma again or you'll have me to answer to.'

'I thought I was doing her a favour.'

'I told you – we can do without favours from you. Is that clear?'

'As crystal. I suppose that applies to the rest of your family?'

'Got it in one.'

The list of people to be checked out seemed to be growing longer by the day. Now, along with Malcolm Forbes's staff and debtors, he had those of Nigel to contend with.

Just to improve his worsening mood, Superintendent Bradley collared him just as he reached the top of the stairs leading to his office.

'Ah, Rafferty. The very man. I presume you were coming to see me with an update?'

'Yes, sir. Of course.'

'Come along then.' Bradley's plump behind led the way. Reluctantly Rafferty followed, mentally rehearsing his excuses.

'Sit down. Sit down,' Bradley invited as he manoeuvred his stout figure behind his desk. 'So. What's been happening?'

'Another loan shark, name of Blythe, has had one of his collectors assaulted. He's in hospital.'

'Another one? How many more are we going to have before you catch the culprits?'

'I'm doing the best I can with limited resources, sir. There's also been a development with the debtors down Primrose Avenue. It seems some of them lied about not seeing Harrison. We have proof of that.'

'Glad to hear you've proof of something, but are you any nearer catching a culprit or two? That's what I want to know – what those at Region want to know.'

That was Bradley all over. Always wanting to shine brightly for the brass, never mind the poor plods at grass level. 'It's a slow process, sir, not helped by not having enough men on the ground. We need to check everything, often several times. But I'm confident we're getting there.'

Bradley harrumphed and muttered something that to Rafferty sounded like, 'I wish I was.'

He tried asking Superintendent Bradley a second time for more officers and came away from the encounter with his ears ringing to the sound of 'precious resources' and 'limited budgets' and 'intelligent usage' of both, with the implication being that he applied intelligence to neither. It was exactly what he'd expected, of course. Bradley had always been one for keeping his officers short of funds for their investigations, the better for his money-management skills to earn him a pat on the head from Region. Solving crimes came a very poor second with that lot unless their egos were scorched by media criticism.

Oh well, he'd tried. Now he'd just have to put his head down and get on with it.

Abra was pleased with the invitations that Llewellyn had done, though Rafferty was careful not to tell her that Llewellyn had produced them and for nothing. Discretion being the better part of valour and all that.

'Where did you get them?'

'Alderton's, the big store in town. They have a special wedding department.'

'Well, I know that. I've been in there enough times. Though I can't say I remember any of these designs.'

'They were new in,' Rafferty quickly responded. 'I popped in earlier.'

'Really? Perhaps I'll go in myself and see what else they've got in new. There might be something I'd prefer.'

'Oh, don't do that, Abra. There's so much to do. Can't we at least get the design of the wedding invitations settled?'

She hummed and hawed for a little, but then said, 'I suppose you're right. It'll be good to get another thing organized.'

'That's what I thought. Which one do you like?' Rafferty asked.

'I think I prefer the jazzy one.'

Rafferty was pleased. 'So do I. So shall I get them ordered? It was two hundred that we wanted?'

'No, of course it wasn't. We're inviting two hundred *people*, not two hundred separate individuals who'd need an invitation each. Most of the invitees are couples or family groups. I've made a list. Order a hundred so we have some spares.'

Abra paused, then she said, 'You know, Joe, when you said you'd take over a chunk of the wedding organization, I had my doubts you wouldn't make a hash of it.'

Rafferty grinned. 'Do you think I didn't know that, my little lemon syllabub? I've hidden talents.'

'Mmm. You must have. Maybe you should try not to keep them so well hidden in future.'

'I'll drink to that.' Rafferty raised his glass of Jameson's and they clinked. 'All my talents will be on show in future.'

'Not quite all, I hope. You don't want to be done for indecent exposure. I don't want the general public seeing more of you than I do these days.'

Rafferty, sensing the complaint that was coming more regularly these days, quickly turned it into a joke to head her off. 'No fear of that. These April nights are too chilly.'

Successfully headed off, after a few seconds Abra told him that, since their last discussion on the subject, she'd plumped for a much more expensive wedding photographer than the one they'd previously agreed on, Rafferty's attempt at hiring the professional who snapped the police bigwigs on special occasions having fallen flat.

'So what was wrong with the other bloke?' Rafferty asked plaintively, thinking that things had gone too smoothly so far this evening. 'The one who did your friend's wedding pictures?'

'Oh, he was all right, I suppose,' Abra replied. 'But you

must look at some of the specimen photos this new photographer gave me. So arty.'

In Rafferty's book 'arty' just meant an excuse to charge more. He wasn't interested in pictures of him and Abra peering soulfully through a romantic mist at their wedding.

He ate his dinner in a morose mood, toying with his food and the idea that he suggested to Abra that they elope together instead. Gretna Green in the moonlight – what could be more romantic? It would certainly be more so than the pile of debts that would await them when they came back from whatever exotic and faraway destination Abra finally settled on for their honeymoon, his attempts at obtaining a freebie holiday having also fallen on stony ground.

To lighten the mood, Rafferty mentioned that Ma had borrowed £500 to buy their wedding present.

Abra was intrigued 'Really?' she said. 'What's she getting us?'

'I don't know. I didn't ask.'

'Oh, Joe! You are hopeless. For a policeman you have a remarkable lack of curiosity. Fancy your mum spending that much. It's got to be something terrific at that price.'

'Mmm. I expect so.' Rafferty had carefully refrained from mentioning that, as he had given Nigel the £500 back, they were effectively buying their own wedding present. He also neglected to mention his suspicion that whatever his ma had bought them would be knocked off.

'I wonder what it is?' Abra continued. 'Do you suppose she'd tell me if I asked her?'

'Doubt it. Anyway, surely it's meant to be a surprise?'

'Oh, pooh! Surprises. Surprises are all very well when you don't know about them. When you do, all they do is get your curiosity roused.'

'You'll have to damp it down till next June then, 'cos I don't suppose Ma'll tell you what it is however much you beg and plead. Ma's a woman well able to keep her own counsel.'

Abra pulled a face. 'Surely she won't expect me to keep my curiosity in check for so long? I'll die.'

'No you won't. You haven't got time to die. There's too much still to do if we're to get everything sorted for the wedding.'

'Oh, you. Aren't you the slightest bit curious?'

'No. Not in the least.' Which was an out and out lie. Though he wasn't so much wondering *what* Ma had got them as much as *where* from and how she'd acquired it. There had been a raid on a local electrical warehouse last week, so maybe the off-the-back-of-a-lorry bargain Ma had bought them was a huge plasma TV. But, like Abra, he'd have to bear his soul in patience till next June. At least, if Ma's present *was* stolen property, the heat would be off it by then.

Abra gave up on the subject and returned to the arrangements for their wedding. As well as the photographer, she had now decided she also wanted his assistant to take a video of the day. All Rafferty saw as he lay down in bed and tried to sleep that night was piles of his hard-earned cash being whisked away from him. And for what? They lived as if they were married already, so it was all for a cheap piece of paper and a couple of wedding bands. Oh, and an album of photographs. He mustn't forget them.

He wondered as he turned over and thumped the pillow if Josie McBride's fiancé was going through a similar trauma. Easy to see why, rather than putting up shelves at his soon-to-be mother-in-law's, he might have struck out at Harrison and all he represented instead. But Anthony Clifford's alibi had checked out. Even one of the mother-in-law's neighbours had backed up his story. At least that saved him the angst of having to arrest a poor sod who was in similar straits to himself.

Twelve

Nigel Blythe had three collectors, including the hospitalized Izzy Barber. Rafferty caught up with one of the other two the next morning just as he was setting out on his rounds.

The man's name was Art Decker, AD to his friends as he told Rafferty, adding, 'but you can call me Mr Decker.'

Decker was built on similar lines to Jaws Harrison and Izzy Barber, though he was about ten years younger than either of the other men and sported gelled spiky hair and a gold tooth that gleamed threateningly in the weak sunlight.

'Well, Mr Decker,' Rafferty began, 'you'll have heard about the local muggings of people in your line of work, one of your colleagues being currently in hospital?'

Decker nodded. The movement made the gold tooth flash blindingly.

Rafferty blinked. 'I wondered whether you could tell me anything about them.'

'Like what? I know nothing about any muggings, apart from the fact, as you said, that Izzy Barber's in hospital.'

'You've heard nothing on the street?'

Decker shook his head. 'I just do my job and go home.'

'You haven't received any threats of violence yourself? Or issued any?'

'No to both. I told you – I just do my job. I don't earn enough to get involved in turf wars on my employer's behalf.'

'So there is a turf war going on?'

'No. None that I know of. It's just that was what you seemed to be implying.'

'You must admit that Malcolm Forbes, one of your boss's rivals in the business, has something of a reputation.'

'I know nothing about that.'

'What about your other colleague, Mr Brian Webb?'

'You'll have to ask him. As I told you, I know nothing about it.' And as he seemed disinclined to say anything more, Rafferty let him go. His colleague, Brian Webb, seemed equally disinclined to say anything useful when Rafferty finally ran him to ground.

Rafferty was frustrated. He'd rarely encountered a case where so many people kept their own counsel or simply lied to him, as he complained to Llewellyn when he got back to the station.

'I suppose you've got to consider the various elements in our investigation: the four youths who seem to have some involvement in both the muggings and the murder; the loan sharks and their collectors; the desperate people who owe them money. All will be inclined to say as little as possible. We're not dealing with cases in a Miss Marple village, but the real world. They're all naturally going to be wary of us and our questions.'

'I suppose so. All I can say is – lucky Miss Marple. Everybody seems to talk freely to her. I wish they'd do the same with me.'

Accompanied by a sporadic drizzle that had washed away the weak sunlight and that although not worth putting up the umbrellas for, nonetheless made their hair and faces wet, Rafferty and Llewellyn returned to Primrose Avenue to see if Jake Sterling or any of his three cohorts were sporting bruises following Izzy Barber's mugging. He'd said his fists had made a couple of connections with faces. For once, the quartet weren't idling their lives away on the street corner.

'Hiding away with their injuries, you reckon, Daff?' Rafferty asked as they parked up and got out of the car. The rain began to fall more heavily as they reached the Sterlings' front door. April was doing its darnedest to live up to its reputation for showery weather.

'Let's wait and see. There's no point in speculating.'

As it happened, Jake Sterling *was* currently sporting some facial injuries; his beaky nose had formed a bloody crust on the tip and the skin around his mouth sported a darkening bruise. Jason, his brother, seemed undamaged. Both appeared subdued, unlike their father.

'Wondered when we'd see you lot again,' he greeted them after Jason had opened the door and led them along to the living room. 'See what some yobs have done to my lads? What are you going to do about it?'

'What happened?' Rafferty asked, going through the motions, though he suspected he already knew how the elder youth had sustained his injuries. The likelihood of the injuries coinciding with the attack on Izzy Barber was too great. Not to mention the coincidence of the Nikes both boys were wearing and the fact that Izzy had said he had been attacked by four youths. Had the attack on Jaws Harrison given them an idea of how to make some easy money? Or had they already been into beating up door-to-door collectors and relieving them of their takings down a convenient alley?

'They were walking through the town centre yesterday afternoon when they were set upon. Tell them,' he insisted as the boys stayed quiet.

'Where was this?'

'On the High Street. Near the Town Hall. About six,' Jake mumbled.

'Should be CCTV footage of the attack then,' Rafferty told him and watched as Jake's face fell. 'I'll get one of my officers to check it out and get back to you.'

'So I should hope,' said Sterling Senior. 'It's coming to something when you can't walk along the street without being attacked.'

Tell that to Izzy Barber, thought Rafferty.

Jake and Jason exchanged a furtive look, but said nothing more.

Rafferty smiled inwardly, sure that their story wouldn't be confirmed by the camera footage. By now, he was convinced they had been in Boadicea Drive mugging Izzy Barber. Shame there were no CCTV cameras there to help him prove it. But both youths, he noticed, had grazed their knuckles, which only added to his belief that their story was a tall one. It would be even more revealing if either Des Arnott or Tony Moran had suffered similar injuries.

He'd had the alley where Barber had been attacked sealed

off and had ordered the SOCO team to check for evidence. The alley would have been muddy from the recent rain so they might get some useful footprints. He studied the boys' Nike trainers more closely. The soles had mud deep in the thick grooves and one of Jake's had what looked like a spot of blood on the toe. Maybe this was one crime that would be quickly solved.

After assuring the three Sterlings that he thought an arrest could be imminent, which led the two youths to exchange another furtive glance, he left, Llewellyn behind him.

'Clearly, they'd forgotten about the CCTV cameras when they told their father they'd been the victims of an assault on the High Street. Should have invented a different location for the attack as their tale puts us in with a chance of proving they're liars.'

Llewellyn nodded. 'Did you see the mud on their trainers? They've been somewhere with soil underfoot recently.'

'Yeah. And last time I looked the High Street wasn't ankle deep in mud. I've a feeling we're about to get lucky on this one. Let's hope they don't have the nous to get rid of their trainers in the meantime.'

'Don't forget we've still to check what Arnott and Moran have to say.'

'I haven't forgotten. But first I want another word with Eric Lewis, the man who found Jaws Harrison's body, seeing as we're in the avenue. I've been meaning to have another chat with him but haven't managed to get round to it. I'll be interested to see if he's come up with another reason why he left it so late after finding Harrison's body to ring it in.'

But when he and Llewellyn turned up at number four, Eric Lewis was still clinging to his story that shock alone had caused the delay.

He was in the family living room. It was a lived-in room, with newspapers and magazines piled on the floor around Lewis's chair. Lewis himself seemed to be starting a cold and seemed pretty sorry for himself. Not wanting to catch his germs, Rafferty sat as far away from him as the living room furniture permitted.

'So why didn't you get someone else to ring it in?' asked

Llewellyn reasonably once they were seated. 'Your wife, perhaps, or one of the neighbours?'

'I don't know.' Lewis waved the question away with a pudgy hand. 'It's all a bit vague now.' He sneezed loudly several times. Groaning, he stretched out a hand to a box of tissues and pulled out a bunch. 'Should you be questioning me when I'm so unwell? I thought there was a law against it.'

'You've only got a cold, Mr Lewis. It's hardly the bubonic plague.'

'Feels like it. My head's thumping something awful. Pass me those painkillers, would you?' He pointed to the mantelpiece, which was decorated with assorted cold remedies.

Llewellyn got up and passed them to him. Lewis shook out three and threw them down his throat, followed by a tot of what looked like hot whiskey.

'Besides, it's only been a matter of days,' Rafferty pointed out. 'I'd have thought such a horrifying discovery would tend to stick in the mind and concentrate one's thoughts.'

'Your mind, maybe, but not mine. Shock's wiped the memory clean away. And this cold doesn't help. Brain feels all foggy. I'm going to go to bed when you've gone. I feel like death.'

Rafferty rather wished his own memory could be so obliging. But even though he pressed the man, Lewis refused to abandon his story.

'Bloody man must remember,' Rafferty complained as he and Llewellyn left the house, slamming the door with unnecessary force behind them, Rafferty hoping it caused Lewis's head to thump even harder. 'He's being wilfully obstructive. I've a good mind to—'

'And what good would that do?' Llewellyn interposed quietly as he correctly guessed Rafferty's thoughts. 'Arresting the man is only likely to make him dig his heels in. He strikes me as the obstinate sort.'

'I know. It's just that sometimes I'd like to break a few rules, go against the restriction on our actions for once and deliver some creative retribution.'

'Just not this evening.'

Rafferty sighed. 'No, not this evening. Come on. Let's get

round to Moran's and Arnott's. I wonder if all four concocted their tale together or whether we're going to get a different version of events from these two.'

As they came out of Eric Lewis's home, they saw Emily Parker leaning on her gate chatting to Jim Jenkins. The weather had improved in the short time since they had left the Sterlings' and now, with the sun released from the earlier heavy bank of cloud, it had turned quite warm. Mrs Parker, freed from the confines of her home by the brightening weather, looked like she was there for the duration.

Rafferty grinned at the expression of resignation Mr Jenkins wore; he'd been buttonholed against his will by an expert and was getting the full flow of her rhetoric by the look of things. Jenkins was leaning heavily on his stick, the odd nod or shake of his head was his only contribution to the proceedings.

Rafferty hurried to the car and got in before Mrs Parker saw them and buttonholed them in place of the hapless Jim Jenkins.

As it turned out, the four youths had had the nous to agree their stories before they shared them, as both Des Arnott and Tony Moran told them the same tale as the Sterling boys. And while Arnott displayed an aggrieved aggression which hinted at impressive acting skills when explaining where and when they'd been 'attacked', Tony Moran seemed shame-faced and reticent, so much so that Rafferty gave him the opportunity to get what had really happened off his chest.

'We have reason to believe your tale's a cock and bull story, Tony,' he told Moran after the youth had repeated the tale of himself and the other three being attacked in the High Street. 'That's not what happened at all, is it?'

'I–I don't know what you mean,' Moran replied, his voice high-pitched and nervous, but seemingly determined not to be the one who blew their alibi for the Izzy Barber assault.

'I think you know very well,' Rafferty told him. 'You weren't anywhere near the High Street, were you? You and your nasty little friends were several hundred yards away, in an alley off Boadicea Drive assaulting one of the debt collectors of a new rival to Forbes. Did Forbes put you up to it?'

Moran said nothing more, so Rafferty told him, 'We're currently getting some forensics from the scene of the Boadicea Drive assault as well as CCTV footage from the High Street where the attack on you and your friends is supposed to have taken place. I imagine the latter, at least, will be revealing.'

Moran shot him a worried look, then he burst out, 'It wasn't my idea. I just sort of tagged along with the others.'

'"The others" being?' Rafferty was keen to be clear on his facts on this one. Although the recent spate of muggings had been carried out on similar lowlifes to the perpetrators, they had been nasty and he would be delighted to see that the perps went down for them. More to the point, so would the superintendent.

'You know who,' Moran muttered. 'I can't say. They'll kill me if I do.'

'Like they killed Jaws Harrison?' Rafferty thought it worth a try to see if Moran admitted to the murder as well.

'No,' he replied sharply. 'We didn't do that one.'

'But you must have a good idea who did. The four of you were there on the spot when Harrison was killed.'

'We saw nothing. None of us had anything to do with that.'

'You're sure?'

Moran nodded.

Rafferty thought he was speaking the truth. 'So tell me about the attack in Boadicea Drive.'

'Ja— my friends,' he hastily corrected himself, 'have been trailing this big bloke for a week or so now. My friend had discovered he was a debt collector. I don't know how, he wouldn't tell me. My friends decided to target him and rob him of his takings. I tried to talk them out of it, but they didn't listen to me. Just called me chicken. They took the piss out of me so much I felt I had to prove myself to them and go along with their plans.'

'Go on. So you followed your victim. What then?'

'Ja— one of my friends said we had to wait till nearly the end of the man's round before we struck so we could be sure of getting a decent haul.'

'So how much did you get?'

'I dunno. Jake— I mean one of my friends took the money. I never saw it. I never even got a penny of it. They said it was my initiation, like, and I had to help in the attack for no more reward than the doing of it.'

'Did you personally assault the victim?'

Moran nodded dejectedly. 'I had to put the boot in once or twice for appearances, like, though I didn't kick him very hard.'

'Somebody did,' Rafferty told him. 'The victim's in Elmhurst General with cracked ribs and a broken jaw as well as internal injuries to his spleen.'

Moran looked even more hangdog at this than he did when Rafferty issued the formal caution. But he still refused to confirm the names of his accomplices.

The youth was more sad than bad in Rafferty's opinion. It was his hard luck that he'd fallen in with the Sterlings and Des Arnott and hadn't the gumption to extract himself from their evil influence. He just hoped Moran admitted the full names of the others involved in the attack for the record; he didn't like to see Moran, the born patsy, going down while the real culprits got off scot-free.

They drove the boy to the station, got his statement – as far as it went – and handed him over to the custody sergeant. And while Rafferty hoped that a stint in the cells would persuade Moran to come clean about his accomplices' identities, he had more urgent matters to deal with than hanging about waiting for the lad to see sense.

Most of those on the latest list of debtors they'd obtained from Malcolm Forbes lived in Elmhurst or the surrounding villages. Forbes apparently liked to be a big fish in a small pond and hadn't done much to extend his loan-sharking operation farther afield. He had a nice little earner locally, so why risk having to mix it with even bigger fish outside his usual area?

The officers assigned to checking out those on the debtors' list were making fair headway. Those of the debtors they had so far checked had alibis that stood up to basic scrutiny, though there were a couple on the list who had relatives on Primrose Avenue. One was a Paul Dicker, the little brother

of Samantha, and the other was the unmarried daughter of
Mr and Mrs Jones. There might yet be others, but the checking
was still continuing and would doubtless go on for some
time yet.

As luck would have it, Paul Dicker and Alison Jones lived
just around the corner from one another in Abbot's Walk and
Cymbeline Way respectively, to the south of the High Street.

Paul Dicker lived in a bed-sit and worked at the DIY store
on the industrial estate. Fortunately, Forbes's list included
telephone numbers. One of the other tenants answered the
phone and told Llewellyn that Dicker was at home, though
he would be going to work shortly, so they went round there
before they missed him, not wanting to cause him any unnecessary embarrassment at his place of work.

Paul Dicker turned out to be a weedy young man in his
late teens. Their appearance agitated him and he explained
he was worried he'd be late for work.

'We won't keep you long, Mr Dicker,' Rafferty assured
him. A quick check on the computer before they left the
station had elicited the information that Dicker had a
conviction for assault. It had happened a year ago when
he, like Tony Moran, had been hanging around with a rough
crowd. He hadn't been in any trouble since and seemed to
have turned over a new leaf since his one and only court
appearance.

Dicker's bed-sit was untidy, like the rooms of most
teenagers. Discarded clothes lay around in heaps and a bag
of clean laundry sat by the door as though its owner expected
it to empty itself into the shabby chest of drawers. There
were posters of footballers and bands decorating the drab
walls; they added a much needed splash of colour in the
otherwise beige room.

Rafferty repeated Llewellyn's telephone explanation for
their visit. 'We're checking with all Mr Forbes's debtors so
that we can narrow down the suspects in our murder investigation. Can you tell me where you were last Friday between
say two forty-five and three thirty?'

'I was at work. I was on the day shift last week. You can
check with my supervisor if you like, Dave Blandford.'

'We'll do that. Thank you. Tell me, Mr Dicker, how are

you coping with your debt to Mr Forbes? Managing to pay it off OK?'

Dicker fidgeted on the unmade bed. His baby face looked pink. 'I've missed a few payments,' he admitted. 'I find it hard to manage since I left home.' He pulled a face. 'My parents split and my mum's married again. I don't get on with her new bloke so I moved out. Sam–Samantha, my sister, tried to persuade me to stay put. She said I wouldn't be able to manage financially on my own.'

It seemed like his big sister had been right, given the loan and the lad's failure to make regular payments.

'Have any threats been made to you regarding your failure to meet your payments regularly?' Rafferty asked.

Dicker went even pinker. 'The collector wasn't very pleasant last time he called. He made it clear he expected me to find the money in future. There was a distinct whiff of "or else" about it. I admit he had me scared. I told my sister what he said.'

'Your sister's in debt to the same firm of moneylenders,' Llewellyn said. 'Do you share the same collector?'

'Yeah. The dead bloke. John Harrison. I was round at my sister's lodgings one day when he called.' He gave a faint smile. 'I thought I'd managed to dodge him at my place, but no such luck. My sister had to make my payment for me. It was good of her as she hasn't much money either. She's a student and she's rarely got any spare cash, so I felt bad about it. She keeps telling me not to worry about paying her back.'

'It must be good to have such a helpful big sister,' said Rafferty, the eldest of six siblings. He wished he had one. 'Makes a habit of getting you out of trouble, does she?'

Dicker nodded. 'I don't know what I'd do without her, especially when it's the end of the month and before I get paid. She always says I ought to live according to my income. That's what she tries to do.' Not with any great success given her association with Forbes. 'She's very frugal. Practically lives on rice and lentils and buys her clothes from charity shops. She says it'll all be worth it when she's qualified and can get a good job.'

Dicker had turned very chatty. He appeared fond of his

sister and it seemed the affection was mutual. Would Samantha Dicker resort to murder to save her baby brother from Jaws Harrison's threats? It was certainly a possibility. Samantha was a strapping girl who clearly made use of all the sporting facilities at the local university. She had told them she rowed for the university team, so wouldn't lack the muscle to attack Harrison. Not that much muscle had been required, according to Sam Dally. Only the element of surprise and the determination to keep hitting.

After confiding his thoughts to Llewellyn once they had left Dicker, Rafferty said, 'Let's get round to this other one on the list, Alison Jones.'

Alison Jones was tall and thin like her mother, but seemed far more animated than the lethargic Margaret Jones. She must take after her father when it came to energy as she rushed about her tiny flat whisking things off seats until the place looked like a whirlwind had gone through it, tidying everything away. Not that it had been unkempt before.

'You said on the phone that you wanted to ask me about my loan.'

Rafferty nodded.

'I suppose it's concerning the murder down my parents' road? They told me about it.'

Rafferty explained they were checking out Forbes's debtors.

'Why? You surely can't think I killed the man? I was at work when it happened.' She reeled off the name and address of her employers, then said, 'I mightn't have liked him, and I've had reason to regret taking out my loan with his firm, but I'm not given to violence.' She faltered suddenly in her confident denial. 'Of course. Silly of me. You've found out, haven't you?'

Rafferty gave an ambivalent nod. Found out what? he wondered. He might not know now, but he guessed that if she was referring to some violent incident in her past, he soon would.

'It was ages ago. I was only a kid. I split a girl's head open when I was in my last year at school. This girl had been bullying me and this one day I just saw red and whacked her with my rounders bat. Problem solved.' She grinned suddenly.

It made her look very like her father. There was a hint of mischief there but also an element of ruthlessness. Problem solved indeed. Did her father share such a character trait? And had he decided on a simple if temporary resolution to his family's problems? If so, would Forbes himself be the next victim?

Thirteen

R afferty was pleased to discover on their return to the station that Tony Moran had decided to come clean and confirm the identities of his fellow assailants. And though he was still adamant that he and his friends had had nothing to do with Jaws Harrison's murder, he admitted they had also been responsible for the other two muggings as well as the one on Izzy Barber. Rafferty, delighted, was hard put to restrain an ear-to-ear grin.

He had the team pick up Des Arnott and the two Sterling youths. He also told them to be sure the three were wearing their leather jackets and Nike trainers, rather than some other unincriminating apparel. It would be good to get the muggings cases, at least, wrapped up.

The three youths were still full of denials and protests of innocence when they were brought in. Followed by yet more 'no comment's. However, they failed even to say the latter when Rafferty ordered them to remove their jackets and trainers. With sneers, they simply slipped out of them as though they believed that any protests would give Rafferty exactly what he wanted.

He rushed the clothing off to the lab for forensic tests with the request that they were processed urgently. Then he went back to the interview room and Jake Sterling.

Sterling looked sullen and not quite so cocky without his leather jacket and sporting the plastic footwear they'd supplied.

'You know your tale about you and your friends being innocent victims of assault is unravelling, don't you?' Rafferty asked.

Sterling said nothing.

'We've got the CCTV footage of the High Street where

you said you and your friends were assaulted. Surprise, surprise, there's not a sign of you, your mates or your assailants. You've been telling porkies, Jake. Not for the first time. So, were you assaulting the opposition for Malcolm Forbes? Putting the frighteners on to encourage the other local loan sharks out of business?'

'No, I wasn't.'

'That's not what your little friend, Tony Moran, said.'

'That little tosser.'

'That little tosser's said some pretty incriminating things.'

'I wouldn't believe a word he says. Little knob still believes in fairy tales. I don't work for nobody, me.'

'Oh, so it was strictly private enterprise mugging you went in for? Is that what you're telling me?'

'I'm telling you nothing. Only that I didn't mug anybody.'

'If that's all you've got to say, you can save it for the judge. I'm confident we've got you for the latest mugging and we've a fair chance on the other two. The forensic results will confirm it. It's only a matter of time, so why don't you confess and make it easier for yourself?'

'Make it easier for you, more like.'

Rafferty looked at him and shrugged. 'Suit yourself. All I was thinking was that a guilty plea would reduce your sentence. You're going down either way.'

But Sterling ignored the advice. As did his brother and Des Arnott. Rafferty left them to stew. He would waste no more time on them. They were guilty of the muggings and he was confident he could at least prove their involvement in the latest one. Maybe, if the lab found traces of Jaws on their clothing, he'd have them for murder as well.

'I reckon we've got them for the Izzy Barber mugging,' Rafferty said after Sterling had been taken back to the cells and he and Llewellyn had returned to the office. 'Maybe even one of the earlier ones if we get really lucky with Forensics, but that still leaves Jaws's murder.'

'I don't think that was one of theirs. Different MO for one thing.'

Rafferty nodded. 'Shame. It would be nice to get these little toughs banged up for some decent time. But I don't think it's going to happen.' Still, he thought, it was good that he'd made such excellent progress on the muggings investigation, as he was due to report to Superintendent Bradley imminently. They'd caught their muggers and all without him really applying himself as diligently as he ought to have done to the case.

'I'm off to get a pat on the head from the super,' he told Llewellyn.

'I wouldn't be so sure,' Llewellyn said. 'We're no further on in solving the murder,' he reminded Rafferty.

'Don't be such a doom and gloom merchant,' Rafferty complained. 'Let me enjoy my moment of triumph. Old Long Pockets Bradley will have forgotten all about it and be on my tail again soon enough.'

'I told you we should concentrate on the psychologies of the suspects. Maybe we can go through them when you return from basking in the superintendent's praise.'

'Maybe.' Rafferty, delighted that his clear-up rate had just improved, was happy to agree to anything. Even a conversation about an 'ology'.

'To get back to the psychological angle we were speaking about earlier,' Llewellyn began when Rafferty returned from having his head reluctantly patted by the super. Llewellyn ignored Rafferty's sigh and went on quietly. 'You have to admit your methods haven't got us much farther forward on the murder inquiry.'

Rafferty was only too aware of it. Hadn't Superintendent Bradley's less than heavy-handed praise for a conclusion to the muggings investigation been interspersed with reproaches for his failure to come up with a solution to Jaws Harrison's killing? 'And there was me thinking I was going about finding the answer in a highly logical manner.'

'You have been,' Llewellyn agreed. 'But you must admit that logic has never been your forte. You've always been better at making wild, intuitive leaps and somehow coming up trumps. Maybe you ought to let the right side of your brain have its head. But while we're waiting for intuition to kick in, now we're reduced to only a handful of suspects having checked the alibis of most of Forbes's debtors, maybe it's time to dig a little deeper into their personalities.'

'OK. Go on, if you must.' Rafferty subsided into his chair. 'Let's hear it.'

'As I said, if we look at the personalities of the remaining suspects, the most likely to my mind are Leslie Sterling and Harry Jones. Though Peter Allbright is still too much of a dark horse to be completely excluded. I—'

The phone went just then and Rafferty snatched it up eagerly. He listened, asked a few questions and put the phone down. 'Well,' he said. 'You're right about one thing at least.'

'And what's that?'

'About Peter Allbright being a dark horse. That was Harry Jones on the phone. Allbright's just topped himself.'

When they got round to Primrose Avenue, it was to find Margaret Jones on the sofa crying softly. Harry Jones was pacing restlessly up and down, as though if he didn't keep active, he too might give way.

'What happened?' Rafferty asked one of the paramedics who'd been called out to attend Allbright.

'Took a load of paracetamol. Late last night would be my guess as he was well gone when we arrived. The empty packets were by his bed. He must have been collecting them seeing as most chemists won't allow you to buy more than sixteen at a time.'

Allbright must have been planning his suicide for some days then. Rafferty wondered if this planning dated back to Harrison's murder. Maybe a count-up of the discarded packets of paracetamol would tell him. But then again, there was nothing to say Allbright hadn't bought all the tablets on the same day at different places.

'We thought he'd gone out this morning when he didn't put in an appearance. Round to the Job Centre,' Harry Jones put in. 'He goes there every day.'

To the chemist's, too, to judge by what the paramedic had said. 'Was there a note?' Rafferty asked, having visions of their murder being solved with Allbright's death confession.

But the paramedic shook his head. 'There was nothing like that. He just upped and left this world without a goodbye to anyone. Didn't leave a thing for his parents or his land-lords to say why he did it. Very sad.'

Even without a note confessing all, Rafferty couldn't help but wonder if this was the solution to the case. Had Peter Allbright killed himself out of remorse for killing Jaws Harrison and the expectation of being arrested?

But when he questioned Harry Jones the man was adamant that neither he nor Allbright had left the garden on the afternoon of Harrison's death. Though, as Rafferty commented later to Llewellyn, he would say that, wouldn't he?

With Harry and Margaret Jones in a state of shock, Rafferty had judged it the right time to question them as to why they had lied about not seeing John Harrison on the previous Friday. But Harry had continued to vehemently deny seeing Harrison. Then Rafferty dropped his bombshell.

'We know John Harrison was here that afternoon,' he told them. 'We have proof. He made a non-payment entry against you and your wife's name and against that of your lodger, so we know he called. So why did you lie about it?'

Slowly, the colour drained from Harry Jones's face till he looked as pale as cream cheese. But this time he didn't deny the accusation. Instead, he just slumped down on the settee which, luckily, was just behind him, and stared at Rafferty with sad eyes, then asked, 'How did you find out? His payment records book wasn't by the body.'

For a moment, Rafferty didn't answer. Instead, he studied Margaret Jones. She didn't seem to have taken in Rafferty's words. She still sat clutching her tissue and staring at nothing. 'We found John Harrison's payments record book. Mr Forbes collected it off Harrison himself and handed it to his accountant. It shows he visited you on the afternoon of his murder. Mr Jones? I'd like an answer, please. Why did you lie?'

The seconds ticked away. Finally, Jones answered. 'I know it looks bad. We knew Harrison's payments book was missing. And given our debt problems, I suppose we just hoped it would never turn up. We took a chance when we said we hadn't seen him that day. But I'm sorry we lied. I suppose it makes us look suspicious?'

Rafferty said nothing for a moment, then, 'No more suspicious than some of the other residents. You're not the only ones who lied to us. But I imagine you already knew that?'

Harry Jones gave a doleful nod.

'How did you know his payments record book was missing?' Rafferty asked. 'It wasn't a piece of information we gave out to the media.'

Harry Jones's brow furrowed. He shook his head. But then his brow cleared and he said, 'I remember now. Eric Lewis must have mentioned it. Him as found the body.'

'We suspected there might have been collusion. Who suggested you all deny seeing Jaws Harrison?'

Jones shrugged. 'I think it was a mutual decision. We were most of us in the same boat.'

'Yet Eric Lewis, who found the body, wasn't in debt to Forbes. Or at least he had all but cleared the debt. Why would he fall in with the story that none of you had seen Harrison that afternoon?'

'I don't know that he did. I'm not even sure that he was aware of our hurried decision. He was in shock, of course, after finding Harrison's body. He said he'd started back up the alley to go home, but before he got there he decided to cross the road to Jim Jenkins's and tell him what he'd found. Emily Parker came out while he was on the doorstep and also heard the tale. After that, it just snowballed down the street. We had a confab here and decided to deny seeing Harrison. It seemed the simplest thing to do. All I can say is that it seemed like a good idea at the time.'

'So who was it who put forward the idea of lying in the first place?'

Jones shrugged.

'Surely you remember? It wasn't that long ago and must have been quite a momentous decision for you all.'

Harry Jones shook his head in a bewildered fashion. 'I don't know. It was all a bit muddled and hysterical. But Margaret and I were just glad to go along with it. We didn't have the money to pay Harrison last week. I know my wife said she had put the money behind the clock, but she hadn't. All she had was an empty envelope. But Harrison had made such alarming threats the last time we couldn't get the money together that all we felt at his death was a kind of respite. That sounds dreadful, I know. But that wretched man hounded poor Peter to take his own life so I can't be sorry he's dead.'

'I'd like to see your lodger's room, please. If you can tell me which one it is?'

Jones nodded. 'It's first left at the top of the stairs.'

Rafferty and Llewellyn went up to Peter Allbright's room. It was the box room. Fortunately, Allbright must have been the tidy sort or the necessity to be tidy had made him so. He hadn't been a hoarder – unless you counted the packets of paracetamol, which he had dropped on the floor after removing their contents. Rafferty had a quick count up. The number of packets tallied with the number of days since Harrison had been murdered. So the deaths were connected, though whether the connection was that Allbright was their killer or just that each day after the murder Allbright had got closer to despair, he didn't know.

He found a diary in the drawer of the bedside table. Rafferty riffled through the pages until he came to the Friday of Harrison's death. But, not unexpectedly, there was no confession on the page. Nor on any of the others. It was just a sad little catalogue of gradually increasing despair and the worthlessness of life.

The other debtors, when questioned about their lies, made similar excuses to Harry Jones. As the old soldier, Jim Jenkins, said when they spoke to him and questioned him about what he knew of the affair, 'If he hadn't been killed when he was, there might have been another death. Another suicide, like Peter Allbright. Maybe with the breathing space his murder has provided, anyone thinking of following his example will think again.'

Rafferty could only hope Jenkins was right.

With Peter Allbright dead and any secrets gone with him, Rafferty and Llewellyn returned to the station to discuss their remaining suspects.

If Allbright *had* been the murderer, it seemed unlikely they would ever prove it. But even with his death the other suspects weren't exonerated.

'I've been thinking,' said Rafferty after a silence of some moments. 'What if our killer bought a new hammer in order to kill Jaws but kept their old hammer and was able to produce it when we hunted for the murder weapon?'

'You're talking serious premeditation.'

'Yes, but there must have been a certain amount of premeditation, surely. Jaws's killer must have lain in wait for his arrival, hammer poised.'

'Well, whether the weapon used was a new one or an old one it's disappeared, so it doesn't much matter either way.'

'Only in so much that as it *has* disappeared we should perhaps be concentrating more on those who left the avenue that afternoon and had the opportunity to get rid of the weapon – the three women: Margaret Jones, Josie McBride and Emily Parker.'

'Of course, it doesn't necessarily mean that one of them committed the murder.'

'No,' Rafferty conceded, 'but it does point to possible complicity by one of them with whoever did kill Jaws.'

Llewellyn nodded slowly. 'Do you want to question the three women again?'

Rafferty shook his head. 'Not yet. I can't see there's much point. They've none of them admitted anything so far. I can't see them doing so now when silence has served them so well.'

'So what *do* you want to do?'

Rafferty pulled a face. 'You tell me. I've been through everything in my mind any number of times and I can't see a way forward. Perhaps something will break of its own accord,' he said with an attempt at optimism.

'Surely it's our job to do the breaking, not to sit around in the blind hope that the fates will do our breaking for us.'

'Go on,' said Rafferty with a scowl. 'Spoil my small stock of hope, why don't you? To turn to another tack. What do you think of Tony Moran's insistence that he and his pals had nothing to do with Harrison's murder?' he asked Llewellyn.

'I'm inclined to believe him. As I said, the MO's not the same. And he's not a very good liar. He admitted his and their involvement in the non-fatal muggings; if he'd had anything to do with the murder I think he'd have been too shocked to tag along behind his friends on another mugging.'

'Mmm. That's your psychological argument, is it?'

Llewellyn opened his mouth to reply, but Rafferty fore-stalled him before he could get a word out. 'As it happens, I think you're right. Though we forgot to ask Moran if he'd seen Leslie Sterling on the street that day. Have we still got him in the cells?'

Llewellyn shook his head. 'Moran and the other three have all been charged and released on bail. Do you want me to have him picked up again?'

'No. Don't bother. I'll pop in and question him again on the way home. I imagine after the day he's had, he'll be lying low in case his friends also want a word.'

Given his lack of conversational skills, Peter Allbright had found an outlet for his feelings about his life, his debts and his inability to get a job in the diary. Rafferty read through it again when Llewellyn had gone off. He could imagine Allbright sitting hunched over in his bedroom pouring all his misery into the diary pages. He read through some more of the entries for the last few weeks and the sense of a growing despair was palpable. Clearly, Allbright's mind had been disturbed enough for suicide. Had it been disturbed enough for murder also?

But no answers came to that particular question. He shut the diary and put it in his desk drawer with a mental reminder to return it to the Joneses so they could hand it and the rest of Allbright's belongings over to his parents. He felt sorry for them when they read it. How would they feel on finding out the extent of their son's desolation? Harry and Margaret Jones were distraught enough and Peter had only been lodging with them.

Had Peter Allbright decided on suicide after the murder, riddled with guilt?

There had been nothing else in the bedroom beyond clothes and a few books and newspapers with job adverts ringed and a concertina file filled with application letters to local businesses that had clearly not even received an acknowledgement. But then such courtesies were rarely gone through now; if you were unsuitable for a job you didn't even get a formal rejection letter more often than not. Your application was just ignored.

The diary had mentioned Harrison's murder, but only briefly. Its purpose seemed chiefly to be the soulmate and best friend, roles that had clearly been lacking in Allbright's empty life.

Rafferty wished he didn't, but, in his bones, he felt convinced that Peter Allbright hadn't been responsible for Harrison's death. Would a man so depressed and deflated be likely to find the spirit or energy for murder? His confidences to his diary had shown just how knocked down by life he had been; certainly, with each rereading of the pages, the main thing that showed through was defeat. There had been no fight left in the man. No, all he had been guilty of was going along with the others when they had decided to lie. And even that had been a half-hearted effort seeing as he hadn't even opened his mouth but had merely nodded or shaken his head in response to each question he and Llewellyn had put to him.

'You know, it's still possible we're on the wrong scent and that someone else had reason other than debt to want Harrison dead,' Rafferty commented when Llewellyn returned with some restorative tea.

'We've no evidence for that,' Llewellyn objected. 'The facts we have point the other way. Few enough could have had the opportunity to kill him without their entry to the alley being spotted.'

'Maybe, but we've only the word of Tony Moran for that. Him and young Bazza Lomond. Moran himself admitted he and his pals were larking about and not always in view of the alley. And Bazza, in spite of what he said about keeping an eye out for Jaws in order to warn his mother of his imminent arrival, was probably paying more attention to his computer game than to what was going on outside his window.'

In spite of Llewellyn's objection, it was certainly a possibility that someone other than one of the Primrose Avenue residents had a motive to kill Harrison, especially given the likelihood that his notebook contained evidence for blackmail. Harrison had spent his life throwing his weight about and threatening those in no position to retaliate; maybe he'd met his match, and his murderer, like Malcolm Forbes, had been another whose visit to the avenue Moran had failed to report to the police, whether from reasons of self-preservation or simply because the alley hadn't been in his view all the time.

But if a potential blackmailee had been Harrison's murderer, they were no further forward in finding out. Rafferty acknowledged that that had been his fault as Llewellyn's limited leisure time had been taken up with producing his wedding invitations. But at least now that job was done. Llewellyn had promised he'd dedicate the few spare evening hours the murder investigation left to him in attempting to decode the notebook they'd found in Jaws Harrison's home.

Rafferty had had another word with Moran on his way home. Like Eric Lewis, Moran seemed to be nursing a cold and also seemed to be feeling sorry for himself.

'You did the right thing, you know, Tony. It's as well that you've confessed to the muggings and incriminated the others. It might just save you from landing in deeper trouble in the future.'

Tony Moran didn't look particularly consoled by this. 'What's going to happen to me?' he asked plaintively. 'I'm scared to go out in case I see Jake and the others. They'll have it in for me for sure. Will I go to prison?'

'You might. These were particularly vicious assaults.'

'But I hardly touched any of them. Only put a kick or two in for form's sake.'

'That doesn't matter. That you were there and involved's enough, though the court might go more leniently on you seeing as you confessed. Take whatever punishment you get as a lesson for the future.' Rafferty paused. 'There was something else I wanted to ask you. Did you see Les Sterling at all on the afternoon of the murder?'

Moran shook his head. 'He'd have been indoors watching the racing. Or up the pub. I didn't see him.'

'Did you see anyone else? I was thinking particularly of Malcolm Forbes. He himself admitted he saw Harrison that afternoon. He came to the alleyway to collect something from Harrison.'

'If he did, I didn't see him. He can't have been there long.'

It wouldn't have taken long to kill Harrison, Rafferty thought. But at least now he thought that Tony Moran had told him the whole truth. And while he admitted to seeing no one else enter the alley, neither did he admit to seeing Leslie Sterling or Malcolm Forbes. They seemed to have reached a stalemate.

Fourteen

But it was a stalemate that was broken the next morning at Llewellyn's triumphant entrance.

'I've managed to decode John Harrison's notebook. It didn't really take very long once I got into it. It was quite a simple code.'

'I suppose it would have to be for Jaws Harrison to concoct it. So what did you find out?'

'That the late Mr Harrison *was* a blackmailer. And that one of his victims is a suspect in his murder.'

'Really? Sounds too good to be true. Which one?'

'One of my preferred suspects. Harry Jones.'

'And what had he done to make him interesting to a blackmailer? Did Harrison's notes reveal that as well?'

'Oh yes. According to Harrison, Mr Jones had been seeing a widow, a Mrs Singleton, on a regular basis. The notebook even supplies the lady's address.'

'Interesting. I did rather wonder how he expended his excess energy given that his wife looks like she'd struggle to find the enthusiasm for supplying conjugals.' Jones had admitted he and his wife were having trouble paying off their loan, so if he was being blackmailed on top of that it could easily be enough to persuade him to violence.

'Want us to go round and have a word with him?'

'No. Not just yet, anyway. I thought I'd try to catch him on his own. He's got enough troubles without me dropping him in it with his wife. Maybe you can give him a bell later and get him to pop into the station?'

Llewellyn nodded.

'I think, in the meantime, we could at least have a word with his lady love, find out how long it has been going on and when Harrison found out about it.'

*   *   *

Mrs Singleton lived in a pretty house in the expensive Dutch Quarter of the town with a view over the River Tiffey. It looked like there was no shortage of money. Had that been part of the attraction for the cash-strapped Harry Jones? Madeleine Singleton was tall and slim like Margaret Jones and around the same age, but any similarity ended there. She was quick in her movements unlike the lethargic Mrs Jones and kept her attractive house looking spruce. The Jones's house, although clean, had shown a distinct lack of homemaking skills, but here, every wall was adorned with paintings, the shelves held books on a variety of subjects and when they called, Mrs Singleton was industriously making a set of blinds on an electric sewing machine. She seemed to have as much energy to spare as Harry Jones. No wonder they'd found mutual satisfaction in expending that energy together.

She didn't try to deny the liaison or act coy when they questioned her about her relationship with Jones.

'We were both lonely, Inspector. We met in the local super-market – Harry always does the shopping – and we just clicked over the cabbages. Rather prosaic, I know. His wife doesn't know about us and I'd rather for Harry's sake that she didn't find out.'

Rafferty nodded and assured her she wouldn't find out from them. 'How long have you and Mr Jones been seeing each other?'

'Six months. It was just after their daughter moved out. I don't think he'd have attempted an affair while his daughter was still at home. Females have a way of sniffing these things out.'

'His wife hasn't.'

'No. But then she's apparently not a very inquisitive woman. She's one of those types who are happy just keeping the house clean and who have no interest in anything else.'

Rafferty thought the judgement a little harsh as Margaret Jones had seemed deeply enough affected by her lodger's sudden death. 'His wife mightn't have found out about your affair,' Rafferty told her, 'but someone did. Did Mr Jones mention to you that he was being blackmailed over it?'

'Blackmailed? No. It's the first I've heard of it. Do you know who by?'

Rafferty nodded. 'I wondered how long the blackmail had been going on.'

'I've no idea. As I said, it's the first I've heard of it. Harry never said anything.' Understandably, she seemed upset about that.

Rafferty had at first believed he should tackle Jones immediately, thinking the shock of his discovery might loosen the man's tongue. But he'd decided against that, merely because if he called him into the station in order to avoid dropping him in it with his wife he would have been on his guard anyway and watchful of what he said. 'I'd like you to speak to him,' Rafferty said now. 'See if you can get him to tell you anything. Will you do that?'

'I'll try.' A fleeting look of awareness crossed her face and she said, 'It was the dead man who was blackmailing him, wasn't it? The one who was murdered down his street?'

Rafferty neither confirmed nor denied it. He and Llewellyn left shortly after, leaving Mrs Singleton looking very thoughtful indeed.

'Do you think she knew Harry Jones was being blackmailed in spite of her denial?'

Rafferty shook his head. 'Doubt it. Though I reckon now she knows it won't take her long to get the truth out of him. Who else can he turn to? And with Harrison dead he might be glad to get it off his chest.'

'Not if he realizes how much more it points the finger of suspicion at him.'

Rafferty nodded sadly. 'There's always that,' he agreed.

Rafferty was called away when they returned to the station and was secluded in a meeting for much of the rest of the afternoon. Llewellyn was waiting for him when he returned to his office with the news that Harry Jones's lady love, Mrs Singleton, had rung up while he'd been otherwise engaged.

'And did she get Harry to spill the blackmailing beans?'

'Unfortunately not. She said he clammed up as soon as she mentioned our visit and refused to be drawn. She said he tried to laugh off the possibility that he was being blackmailed over their affair, though, according to Mrs Singleton, he didn't manage it very successfully.'

'Maybe it's time we had a word with him ourselves. Did you contact him as I asked?'

'Yes. He's coming in later this afternoon.'

'Has the team dug up anyone else on Forbes's long list of debtors who has relatives on Primrose Avenue?'

'Not yet. But of course the names of any debtor relatives aren't always the same as those of the residents, which doesn't make the job any easier, especially if the debtors fail to inform us of any family connection.'

'Keep them at it as we seem to be going nowhere very fast on this one.' If he didn't find the culprit soon he'd be forced to take up Llewellyn's suggestion of looking at the psychological angle. But he couldn't see that taking them further forward. After all, Llewellyn's favourite suspects had been Leslie Sterling, Harry Jones and Peter Allbright. And they already knew that Sterling appeared a selfish scrounger who'd slit his granny's throat for a betting stake. And as for Harry Jones – the man had shown himself capable of deception in carrying on with the widow Singleton for six months. Who was to say of what else he might be capable? And Allbright was a defeated suicide with no energy for life, never mind murder. Such conclusions hadn't required any great psychological insight. But unless Jones cracked when they interviewed him they would be no further forward apart from having a second motive for the man to go alongside the original one.

As soon as Harry Jones was shown into Rafferty's office, before he had even taken a seat, Rafferty threw down Jaws Harrison's notebook, open on the page that referred to Jones's affair with Mrs Singleton, then threw Llewellyn's decoding of its contents down after it and said, 'You didn't mention the dead man was blackmailing you.'

Harry Jones was remarkably calm. But then he'd had time to get used to the idea that they knew of his predicament, as, presumably, Mrs Singleton had told him from where she'd obtained the information. He sat down and looked Rafferty in the eye before he replied. 'I was being blackmailed, yes. But how was I to know it was Jaws Harrison doing the black-mailing? I didn't. I never even got to speak to him. He mailed me the evidence he had of dates and times I spent with Madeleine. He even sent incriminating photos of us kissing on her doorstep. And I sent him the money he demanded via a post office box. It could have been anyone I knew. I had no more reason to kill him than any of the others had.'

'And why should I believe you? You've done nothing but lie to me and keep things from me.'

'I'm not the only one who lied to you.'

'No, but you're the only one who had an additional reason beyond your debt to Malcolm Forbes to want Harrison dead.'

'I told you, I didn't know it was him who was the black-mailer.'

'So you say. So how long had he been putting the screws on you?'

'A couple of weeks.'

And within less than a fortnight Harrison had been murdered. It was pretty damning whatever Jones might say about not knowing or guessing the identity of the blackmailer. 'How much did you pay him?'

'Five hundred pounds.' He pulled a face. 'I got another loan out.'

'So you're deeper in the mire than ever, then?'

'What choice did I have?' Jones burst out. 'I can't get a job. I'm already up to my ears in debt that I'm having diffi-culty in repaying. What difference does a bit more make? I'm in Queer Street anyway and at the end of my tether. Seeing Madeleine Singleton was the only thing that gave me any joy to compensate for the rest.' He hesitated and then said, 'You–you're not going to tell my wife about our affair?'

Rafferty thought it would serve him right after his lies if he did so. But as Jones had said, he was clearly unable to take much more strain. He didn't want another Peter Allbright on his conscience. 'No,' he said. 'I won't tell your wife. But if there's anything else you've been concealing from me, I want to know now. Is there anything?'

Harry Jones shook his head. 'There's nothing else. I've told you everything. Can I go now?'

'Yes.' Rafferty nodded to Llewellyn who was sitting at his own desk in the corner taking notes. 'Perhaps you'll escort Mr Jones from the premises?'

When Llewellyn and Harry Jones had gone, Rafferty stared down at Harrison's incriminating notebook and the sheets containing Llewellyn's cracking of his code, but he didn't see the words written on it. All he could see was a case that was still going nowhere. Even if Jones *had* killed Harrison they had no evidence to prove it.

Rafferty's phone rang then and he snatched it up, ever hopeful of some new piece of evidence come to light. But it was only his ma.

'What do you want, Ma? I'm busy.'

'Sure and you're always busy. But not too busy to speak to your mammy. Besides, I've a piece of news I thought might interest you.'

'News? What news?'

'Sure and it can wait a minute while you ask how I am and how the rest of the family are. What's happened to your manners, son? I didn't teach you to speak to people like that.'

'Sorry, Ma. How are you?'

'My veins are playing up a bit. My legs are throbbing.'

'Put your feet up then and take it easy.'

'That's what I'm doing. Though it's annoying me. You know how I hate to be idle. I was going to take down the living room curtains and give them and the windows a good wash.'

'Don't you go climbing on chairs, Ma. I'll take them down next time I come round. Surely there's no rush?'

'I like to keep a clean house. Not like some.'

Him, he supposed. He judged it safe now to return to the news she had spoken of. 'You said you had something for me, Ma. What was it?'

'A little bit of gossip from the neighbourhood I thought would interest you. Mrs Parker of Primrose Avenue told me.'

Told you what? he felt like demanding. But he kept his cool. Ma liked to string her stories out.

'You'll never guess.'

'I don't think I will, Ma, so why don't you just tell me?'

There was a sigh from the other end of the line. 'Oh, go on then. She told me that Malcolm Forbes had sent his men around her street questioning the residents and—'

'Questioning them?'

'That's what she said.'

'What were they asking?'

'What they'd seen and heard. If they had any suspicions of anyone in particular.'

'They didn't issue any threats?'

'She didn't say so. Though I suppose they might have done as they were a couple of big bruisers from what she said. Though I don't suppose they suspected Emily Parker of attacking the man so they would hardly need to threaten her.'

'Thanks, Ma. That's interesting. Could be useful.'

'That's what I was thinking. Anyway, son, I'll let you get on. I just thought I'd tell you the latest.'

'I appreciate it, Ma. Thanks again. Bye for now.'

He replaced the receiver as Llewellyn returned and asked, 'What did you think of what Harry Jones had to say?'

Rafferty gave a wry grin. 'For what it's worth, I don't think he's our killer. Do you?'

Llewellyn, never one to breezily brush aside a piece of evidence, said, 'I don't know. I think I'd prefer to reserve judgement on that one.'

Rafferty sighed again. 'I suppose you're right. His wife is certainly one of the few suspects who could have disposed of the murder weapon.'

'Maybe we should have her in?'

'Maybe we should.'

He was at a loss as to what else they could do. They'd interviewed all the suspects several times, caught a number of them out in lies, but were still no further forward. The checking out of Forbes's and Nigel Blythe's debtors' lists were ongoing and would be for some time, though, truth to tell, he'd no great hopes from that avenue and considered it more a straw-clutching exercise than anything else.

To take his mind off the frustration the investigation was causing, he changed the subject and said to Llewellyn, 'I've been meaning to ask you how your studies are going for your inspector's exams.'

'I'm taking my studies slowly and getting one element thoroughly learned before I embark on the next. I'm in no hurry. Better to pass first time than fail and have it all to do again.'

Rafferty nodded. It was so like Llewellyn's approach to everything: slow, thorough and painstaking. So different from his own erratic and occasionally inspired efforts. Llewellyn had begun studying around the time he'd met and married Mo, his intellectual, blue-stocking wife, who was also a cousin of Rafferty. He was often amazed at the different results brought about by the same family gene pool. He had no doubt that Llewellyn would pass his inspector's exams at the first attempt. He was methodical, although his cool, logical approach sometimes drove Rafferty to distraction. Strangely, in view of their markedly different approaches, they worked well together, each supplying what the other lacked, with Rafferty's impulsiveness curbed by Llewellyn's stern logic and Llewellyn encouraged to approach things from one of Rafferty's often off-beat angles. So far in their investigations the combination had stood them in good stead. Rafferty was hopeful it would do so again on this one.

'By the way, I forgot to tell you in all the excitement about the blackmail. I heard from Ma that Forbes has sent around a couple of his minions to question the residents of Primrose Avenue. Must have decided to conduct his own investigation – unless he's the guilty party and is putting the frighteners on any potential witnesses.'

'Maybe we should warn him off? If he's intimidating witnesses—'

'On what evidence? Ma's say-so? Anyone who knows anything will clam up from fear of what he might do if they let anything slip. If they know anything. God knows they haven't exactly been founts of knowledge over this murder so far. Though I suppose we could put tails on Forbes's men for a few days, if the budget will stand it, and see if they pay a return visit to the avenue. Put the frighteners on *them* for a change.'

'Is there any point in that?' Llewellyn questioned. 'I would have thought any possible damage has already been done. If anyone did remember something they'd be certain to have forgotten it after a visit from Malcolm Forbes's thugs.'

'I suppose you're right. OK. Let's put the frighteners on

Forbes himself. Threaten to do our best to get his licence revoked.'

'Again – on what evidence? That of Bazza Lomond, that reputed teller of tall tales?'

'Let's try anyway. What harm can it do?'

'Plenty, I would think. His solicitor might issue a harassment suit. I can imagine what Superintendent Bradley would say about that.'

So could Rafferty. He scowled as he was reminded of Forbes's legal bogeyman. Stymied from action on the Forbes front by Llewellyn's irrefutable logic, Rafferty admitted a temporary defeat. If his witnesses had been got at, as Llewellyn said, it was too late to do anything about it now. But that was no reason not to go and see Forbes and let him know that they were aware of his interference in the case.

Margaret Jones, when they had her in the station for questioning, was very vague and still inclined to be weepy about the death of her lodger.

'Why are you asking me all these questions?' she demanded at one point. 'I've already answered most of them once.'

'You know why, Mrs Jones. Did your husband or Peter Allbright murder Jaws Harrison? Did you dispose of the weapon?'

'Me? Of course not. According to what I've heard it was a hammer that was used to kill him. Ours isn't the only hammer on the street. Besides, it's still in the shed.'

'That's as may be, but very few people left the vicinity of Primrose Avenue after the murder and had the opportunity to dispose of the weapon before Uniformed police arrived. You're one of them.'

'Our hammer's not even missing,' she insisted again. 'You know that. You had your officers check through Harry's toolbox and the shed.'

Rafferty nodded, acknowledging her point. But then, with the lack of security on the neighbourhood's sheds, anyone could have helped themselves from any of the avenue's shed contents. The fact that the Joneses' hammer was still on their premises proved nothing.

'Why are you so sure it was a hammer, anyway? If you can't find the weapon you surely can't be certain what it was that caused Mr Harrison's injuries.'

It was a valid point. One Rafferty hadn't expected from Margaret Jones. Sam Dally had simply said the weapon had either been a hammer or something like a hammer. Something with a metal end, anyway.

'Can I go now? Mrs Jones asked plaintively.

She might as well, Rafferty thought as he gave her the nod. She'd told him nothing useful. In fact the only witnesses to tell him anything at all helpful had been Tony Moran and Bazza Lomond and the information from the tall-tale telling Bazza couldn't be relied upon, though it was unfortunate that Bazza hadn't seen what Malcolm Forbes had been carrying when he came out of the alley.

There was nothing for it but to have Tony Moran in again and put the fear of God into him. He'd been nearer to the end of the alley than Bazza. Maybe Moran would finally be persuaded to admit to seeing Forbes and had seen what the loan shark had been carrying. Rafferty just hoped the youth was more afraid of him than he was of Forbes or his three thuggish mates.

But before he spoke to Moran again he had someone else he had to see as a matter of urgency.

'Hold the fort for me,' he instructed Llewellyn as he shrugged into his jacket and raincoat. 'I've got to go out. One of my sources rang up while you were collecting Margaret Jones from reception.'

Rafferty's snout, Stinky Harold, to judge by the smell of him, must spend most of his time on the council's rubbish dump. He met him on the stairwell of the grey, dank and entirely uninviting top floor of the multi-storey. Making sure to stand well downwind of his snout, Rafferty said, 'So what have you got for me, Stinky?'

'Something worth ten of your Earth pounds,' Stinky replied.

This was something of a running gag between them as Stinky was so other-worldly he might as well be an alien. He was a small man who wore numerous layers, each succeeding layer a little cleaner and less torn than the preceding one. Like Rafferty, he was originally from London. His accent was pure 'sarf' London.

'I'll be the judge of that,' Rafferty told him. 'So, come on, out with it. What have you got?'

'It's to do with The Enforcer, Malcolm Forbes. Word on the manor is that he's had his blokes questioning the people on Primrose Avenue.'

Rafferty had hoped for something more than information that his ma had already supplied for nothing. 'Is that it?' he asked. 'Where did you hear this anyway?'

Stinky tapped his nose. 'Can't reveal my sources, Gov. But it's kosher. God's troof.'

'Has he been threatening them or simply trying to extract information on any possible murderer so he can obtain his own revenge and show himself as the hard man?'

'I don't know. But any visit from them blokes seems like a threat to those on the receiving end. Reckon he killed that bastard, Jaws, for reasons best known to himself and wants to make sure any evidence is silenced at birth?'

'As to that, we'll have to see.' Rafferty pulled a ten pound note out of his wallet and handed it over, careful to hold on to just the corner so he didn't accidentally touch Stinky's grimy hand.

The tenner quickly disappeared into one of the folds in Stinky's multi-layered clothing. He immediately slunk away, leaving only a pungent odour behind him.

Feeling he'd wasted a tenner and time he couldn't spare, it was a disgruntled Rafferty who headed for his car and the station.

When he got back to the station and told Llewellyn that his ma's story had been backed up by his snout, he said, 'I reckon we should question the residents again. Surely one of them will let slip whether they were warned off or merely questioned. We need to know, one way or the other.'

Llewellyn nodded.

'After that, I think another visit to Forbes is called for.'

But before they could do either, Llewellyn had some news for him.

'An anonymous phone call has come into the incident room,' Llewellyn told him.

'What did it say?'

'That Les Sterling had a big argument with John Harrison a week before he died.'

'Strange that none of his neighbours reported it. They might well have thought it a good way to put someone else firmly in the frame.'

'Mmm. I wondered that. I also wondered whether the anonymous call mightn't have been made by someone with a grudge against Mr Sterling. He's not the most personable of men. He also has two loutish sons who regularly make nuisances of themselves in the neighbourhood.'

'Only one way to find out: let's go and have a word with the very unpersonable Mr Sterling and see if he denies it. If he starts blustering there might just be something in it.'

Fifteen

L es Sterling was out when they called at his home, but his wife was in. Mrs Sterling was a small, thin woman who wore a harassed expression. But then, with the shiftless Les for a husband and two unruly sons, she had a lot to look harassed about.

'Where is your husband, Mrs Sterling?' Rafferty asked as she held on to the door as if for support.

'He's gone up the bookies.'

'Do you mind if we come in and wait for him? It's important.'

She let go of the supportive door frame with a defeated air and stood back. She was more hospitable than her husband and offered them tea while they waited.

Rafferty nodded and smiled his thanks. At least the tea would help the time pass till Les Sterling deigned to put in an appearance.

It was clear Mrs Sterling was a browbeaten woman with little to say for herself. After she brought the tea in, she sat down on the edge of an armchair and kept darting anxious little glances at them.

Rafferty took it upon himself to break the ice. 'You make a lovely cup of tea, Mrs Sterling.'

She gave him a quick, nervous smile, but said nothing.

'Tell me. Did you know the victim, Mr Harrison, at all?'

She shook her head. 'It was Les who got in touch with his firm.'

'Did he consult you about taking out this loan?'

Her thin face seemed to become thinner. 'No. He never consults me about anything. He always says that if a man can't be boss in his own house it's a poor do. I was horrified when I found the paperwork for the loan. Such a lot of money. How we're to repay it, I don't know.' She looked as if she might cry. 'I wish he hadn't done it. We'd be able to manage on my wage if he didn't drink, smoke and gamble. I'll have to put in for some more overtime if we're ever to clear it.'

She looked thin enough now, thought Rafferty. What would she look like after she spent months putting in even more overtime than she must currently be doing? She'd wear away to nothing. But it was unlikely her husband would bestir himself and get a job when his wife made such a doormat of herself.

Just then, the front door slammed and seconds later, the unkempt figure of Les Sterling appeared in the doorway.

Immediately he saw them his face turned thunderous and he began to berate his wife. 'What the hell do you think you're doing, you stupid cow, letting coppers in the house when I'm not here?' He strode into the room and stood menacingly in front of his wife, who cowered back in her chair, spilling her tea in her lap and staring up at her husband in fear. 'What have you told them?'

'I–I haven't told them anything, Les.'

'You better not have.' He raised his hand threateningly. 'Or—'

'Why don't you sit down, Mr Sterling, instead of threatening your wife in front of witnesses?'

Sterling scowled at him. 'Don't you tell me what to do in my own home, copper. I do what I like.'

'So it would seem. Like having a flaming row with the dead man?'

Sterling stared stupidly at him for a moment. 'What?'

'We've a witness who swears they saw you having a stand-up row with Jaws Harrison. Are you telling me you didn't?'

'Yeah. That's exactly what I'm telling you. Bleeding cheek. You come into my home with your lies, frightening my wife and—'

'It seems to me, Mr Sterling, that the only person frightening your wife is you. Why don't you sit down and calm down?'

''Cos I don't choose to, that's why.' He marched to the door. 'I want you out of my house.' He yanked the living room door open. 'Now. You come here, making insinuations and—'

'No insinuations, Mr Sterling. I merely asked you a question as part of a wider murder investigation. You said you didn't have a row with the deceased. Fine. That's all I wanted to ask you. If you say you didn't have a row with Mr Harrison, I have to believe you. For the moment, anyway. Of course, I'll be making further enquiries in the neighbourhood to try to find out if you're telling me the truth.' Rafferty stood up. 'We'll see ourselves out.'

They heard Sterling lambasting his wife as they shut the front door behind them.

'Poor bitch,' said Rafferty. 'She must lead a dog's life with him and their two charming sons.'

Llewellyn nodded. 'And now they have a large debt to add to the brew.'

'If the woman had any sense, she'd leave him and his large debt to stew, but I don't suppose she will. The years of browbeating and bullying have clearly taken their toll.'

'We each make our own troubles in this life,' was Llewellyn's philosophical response. 'Do you think Mr Sterling was telling the truth?'

'No. Do you?'

Llewellyn shook his head.

'That being the case, why don't we make a start on questioning his neighbours again? The ones either side of him seem favourite to me.'

So saying, Rafferty opened the gate of the Sterlings's next-door neighbour, walked up the path and knocked on the front door.

His knock was answered by a woman with a flowery pinny and floury hands.

'Yes?'

'Good afternoon. Mrs Palmer, isn't it?'

'That's right. You're the policemen investigating the murder, aren't you?'

Rafferty nodded. 'I wonder if we could come in for a few minutes? There's something I'd like to talk to you about.'

'Yes, of course. Come in. I'll just wash my hands.' She

led them into the living room. 'Sit yourselves down. I won't be a moment.'

She was soon back. 'Now,' she asked, as she sat down, 'how can I help you?'

'We've received information that your neighbour, Mr Sterling Senior, had a big argument with the man whose murder we're investigating. I wondered if you'd heard this row?'

She shook her head. 'I don't think so. When is it supposed to have happened?'

'The Friday before the murder.'

'Oh. I remember now. My husband did mention something. I didn't take a lot of notice. Les Sterling's the sort of man who rows with everyone. We must have had half a dozen rows with him since we moved in a year ago. Usually about those sons of his. I feel sorry for his wife. Nora seems really cowed. I've had her in here in tears before now.'

'You said your husband heard Mr Sterling arguing with someone. Are you sure it was the Friday before the murder?'

'Yes. Because it was our day for fish and chips. We always have fish and chips on a Friday. My husband works shifts and he was on earlies that day so we had a late lunch. But I don't know who he was arguing with. My husband never said. And I wasn't that interested.'

'We'd like to speak to your husband. If we return this evening is he likely to be at home?'

'Yes. We've no plans for going out.'

They had to leave it there. They thanked her and left.

'Let's try the neighbours on the other side,' Rafferty said. 'We might strike even more lucky.'

But the neighbours on the Sterlings's other side were unable to help. Neither of them had been in on the Friday before the murder so had heard nothing.

'Oh, well,' said Rafferty as they got in the car to drive back to the station. 'We'll just have to bear our souls in patience and wait till this evening.'

Les Sterling was standing in his doorway watching them with a brooding air as they drove away. His sullen face wore a hard-done-by expression that would have been funny if it wasn't for the fact that the way he went inside and slammed the door behind him boded ill for his wife.

When they returned to Primrose Avenue that evening to speak to Mr Palmer, they were waylaid at the gate by Les Sterling. He looked a bit hangdog.

'You'd better come in. I don't want that bastard next door badmouthing me.'

He led the way into his living room. He even invited them to sit down.

There was no sign of Mrs Sterling or his sons. Had they been banished so Les could unburden himself in private?

'The thing is,' Sterling began, 'I *did* have a few words with Jaws Harrison. The bastard had been trying to cheat me, hadn't he.'

'Cheat you?' Rafferty repeated. 'In what way?'

'He took the money I paid off the loan, but he didn't enter the payments. I only found out when I contacted the office and asked for an up-to-date statement.'

'I see. And you had it out with Mr Harrison?'

'Too right, I did. It's hard enough making the payments without being cheated out of those you do make. Bastard's lucky I didn't knock him into next week.'

'Did he admit it?'

'Didn't have to. I snatched the payments record book off him and shoved it under his nose. I knew I'd made those payments and so did he.'

'Did you complain to the office?'

'Course I bloody complained. What do you take me for? I told that Forbes his man was a tealeaf. He tried to make out I was a liar. I'd no proof, of course, as I paid Harrison in cash from my betting winnings. It was my word against his, wasn't it? Bastard. Even so, I tell you I was surprised when my boys told me they saw him again the next Friday, bold as brass. He never came here; must have been murdered before he finished across the way. He should have been sacked for what he did to me and so I told his boss. But people like that, they're all crooks, robbing innocent folk. I told Forbes, I said, I won't be taking another loan out with your lot. Not after this. He said he'd look into it, but he can't have done, can he? Not when Jaws turned up again the next week, large as life.'

It was clear that Les Sterling was a man with a grievance, though whether it was a justified one or just Sterling attempting and failing to try it on in order to get out of making a few payments, was debatable.

One thing, though, as Rafferty told Llewellyn once they'd finally escaped Sterling and his hard-done-by tale, it gave Forbes the strong motive for murder that they'd been lacking before. Of course it also gave the aggressive Les Sterling good reason to want to do Harrison serious damage.

'Though I can more easily imagine Sterling punching him in the face at the time of the row than creeping up behind him an entire week later and bashing him on the head. Not a man to defer his pleasures, our Leslie.'

'Mmm. Doesn't quite seem Forbes's style, either.'

'Don't say that!' Rafferty protested. 'We get a new piece of evidence that points the finger at two of our favourite suspects and here we are doing our damnedest to exonerate them both. Let's not go there. One thing, anyway, if Sterling killed him it would explain the theft of Harrison's wallet and collection money. Come on, let's get this meeting with Mr Palmer over and then we'll call it a day. It's been a long one.'

Their meeting with Mr Palmer didn't take above five minutes. He confirmed, as far as he was able, from what he had overheard, what Les Sterling had told them.

The next day, Rafferty, feeling surprisingly full of renewed vigour, decided to widen other lines of enquiry. For, as he told Llewellyn, there were a couple of areas they had neglected to look into very deeply: one, the possibility of a turf war having broken out, with Jaws Harrison and Izzy Barber its victims, along with the other two men who had been the earlier victims of assault. The other thing he wanted to dig deeper into was the possibility that the two young women involved in the case, Samantha Dicker and Josie McBride, might not be as innocent as they claimed.

He had mainly dismissed them as suspects as he hadn't seen the murder as a woman's crime; the likelihood of either young woman being guilty of an attack on the brick outhouse that had been Jaws Harrison had seemed unlikely in the extreme. But in a murder investigation even the extremely unlikely must be delved into. To this end, he set two of the team to delving into the young women's pasts.

At first, they didn't discover anything, but as they dug deeper and questioned the moneylenders in the area, they heard a curious tale: that Josie McBride wasn't quite the innocent young woman she had been thought to be.

She had taken out a loan several years earlier with a rival firm to Forbes and had been accused of assaulting the collector when he had called for her latest instalment. No charges had been brought and it had gone no further, so the assault couldn't have been a serious one. Even so, it revealed there was more to Josie McBride's character than had previously been suspected.

'Not so butter-wouldn't-melt,' Rafferty commented. 'Maybe she took exception to Forbes's collector, too? Did the team find out why she assaulted the earlier collector?' he asked Llewellyn.

Llewellyn nodded. 'It seems he made improper suggestions to her.'

'Improper suggestions? How very old-fashioned. I suppose you mean he said that if she slept with him he'd knock a chunk off the debt?'

'Just so.'

'Who'd have thought such things would go on in this day and age when young women seem to drop their drawers obligingly on the slightest acquaintance. Did Lizzie Green question Ms McBride about the incident?'

'Yes. She said all she did was slap the man across the face. It didn't hurt him. She said he laughed at her and went away still chuckling.'

'And who was this collector?'

'None other than Izzy Barber. He was working for Dean Everitt, another moneylender, at the time.'

'Well, well. What a small world we move in, to be sure. He seems to suffer particularly badly from the occupational hazard of being assaulted – hardly efficient when he and his ilk are meant to dole out the punishment. I shouldn't wonder if cousin Nigel doesn't regard him as surplus to requirements, with hospitalization a sackable offence. Thoroughly deserved, I'm sure.' He broke off, then asked, 'Any news on the turf war aspect?'

'Not as yet. But I instructed the team to put further feelers out. Hopefully, if there's anything in it, we'll hear shortly.'

Rafferty nodded. 'Let's have another word with Izzy Barber.'

They got over to the hospital. Barber was looking marginally better but clearly feeling a lot more sorry for himself and consequently more inclined to let something slip. He went as far as to admit that there *had* been bad feeling between Nigel Blythe's collectors and those of Malcolm Forbes.

'There was a certain resentment between the two teams,' he said. 'An antagonism. But it was an antagonism of words only,' he added at the spark of interest in Rafferty's eye. 'Not of action.' He was insistent on this last.

Given Jaws's death and Barber's assault and hospitalization, Rafferty wasn't sure he believed him. He thought it possible that both investigations – the murder and the muggings – might, after all, have been the result of this antagonism.

More determined now to discover the truth, he set the team to questioning those who frequented the local pubs that Izzy Barber, his colleagues and those of Jaws Harrison favoured. Gradually, there seeped back to him the news that Barber and his colleagues hadn't denied an involvement in Jaws's death.

It might, of course, merely be bravado on their part. A message sent out to the opposition that they were to be treated with respect.

Rafferty wasn't sure. It was still possible that Jake Sterling and his three friends had been responsible for Jaws Harrison's murder. That didn't necessarily preclude the possibility that they had been put up to it by Forbes himself.

The trouble was that he still had no proof. He had proof of precious little apart from Tony Moran's confessions about the muggings, and all these investigations into feuds and vendettas were taking up valuable time and man hours that should have been devoted to the core of the investigation.

It was a continuing frustration that seemed to have no end. He was weary of it.

Interrupted by the news about Les Sterling's argument with Jaws Harrison, Rafferty's previous plans had been rather put out of kilter. But now he resurrected them.

Once they were in the car and on the way, Rafferty said, 'I think we'll question Mrs Emily Parker first. As she's the street's nose for gossip we might get more out of her than the rest.'

As it turned out, Mrs Parker was unable to help them. 'Visitors?' she asked. 'Visitors from Mr Forbes?' She shook her head. 'I've not seen anyone. No one's been round to ask me questions, though I know they questioned some of the neighbours. Maybe they missed me? I was round my daughter's for several hours yesterday.'

Having drawn a blank, they took their leave and tried Josie McBride. She admitted that she'd had a visit from a couple of men.

'What did they say?' Rafferty asked.

'Very little. They seemed pretty cagey.'

'Were they threatening at all?'

'No. They simply asked me if I'd seen anything and what I'd told you. I told them the same that I told you – that I'd seen and heard nothing – and they went away.'

They questioned the other residents again, but they all said the same as Josie McBride.

'Seems Forbes wasn't getting his men to put the frighteners on them after all,' said Rafferty as they drove back to the station. 'Sounds like he decided to do some investigating of his own.'

'There's no law against it.'

'More's the pity. I don't like him conducting his own investigation. I wouldn't want him to discover something we missed and rub our noses in it.'

'That doesn't seem likely in view of what the residents said. Besides, it would be better if *someone* discovered some new evidence.'

Rafferty just gave a reluctant nod to this. 'Let's pay him that visit, anyway. Let him know we don't like our turf being invaded any more than he does.'

* * *

Malcolm Forbes didn't even bother to make them wait while he fielded his brief. He merely bid them a good afternoon and asked what they wanted.

'I hear your men have been questioning the residents of Primrose Avenue,' Rafferty told him. 'And I want to know why.'

Forbes stretched against the high back of his leather chair. His hands rested idly on the arms as he said, 'The fact that one of my men has been murdered's not reason enough?'

'No. Questioning witnesses and suspects is *my* job, Mr Forbes, not yours. We'll find out who killed Mr Harrison. We don't need your help.'

Forbes merely laughed as if he found this declaration amusing. 'So you don't want to know what my men found out?'

Rafferty would have preferred to say 'no', but he couldn't allow himself the luxury of hubris. 'OK,' he said. 'Tell me. What did they find out?'

'Only that one of Harry Jones's sons makes a habit of climbing over the factory wall that backs on to the avenue mornings, evenings and at lunchtimes to go home. Saves walking round the long way.'

That would be Billy, the younger son who worked at the canning factory.

'Maybe he climbed over at other times, too, and did more than go for a bacon butty.'

'And who told you that?'

Forbes was beginning to look bored by the conversation. 'Do we really need to go into that?' he asked. 'The last thing I want is to get anyone into trouble.'

'You seem happy enough to drop one of the Jones boys in it. Anyway, let me worry about that.'

Forbes shrugged his meaty shoulders. 'Very well. I understand it was one of the kids who live in the street. At number nine, I believe. I don't know the brat's name.'

Number nine was Tracey Stubbs's place. Forbes had supplied them with an interesting piece of information. If it was true. He thanked Forbes and left his pawnbroker's shop, followed by Llewellyn. This information opened yet another line of investigation.

'Let's go and see Tracey Stubbs and her brood and see what we can learn,' Rafferty said. 'Like why her kid didn't see fit to give us this piece of information.'

Tracey Stubbs was in the middle of a big wash when they called – getting the kids' school uniforms and sports kits ready for the new term.

The house was as much of a tip as it had been the last time they'd called. In the kitchen, a pile of grubby white shirts and blouses awaited their turn in the washing machine. It was currently going through the spin cycle and making one hell of a racket. A tumble dryer was also on the go.

Rafferty was always amazed that people on benefits seemed able to afford all the gadgets. He didn't have a tumble dryer because they ate money, yet young Tracey was clearly able to afford one. He wished he knew how she did it. He gestured to her that they should go into the living room and shut the door behind them to keep the noise in.

'That's better,' he said, as he, Tracey and Llewellyn settled on chairs. 'We've been having a word with Malcolm Forbes,' Rafferty told her. 'And he said that one of your children claims to have seen the younger Jones boy climb over the factory wall. I gather he makes a regular habit of it. I wondered if you knew which of your children told Forbes's men this?'

She nodded. 'That'll be Danny. I heard the bell ring. He answered the door to them and must have been speaking to them for a while before he called me.'

'Could we have a word with him? We won't keep him long.'

'Sure. Why not? I'll call him.' She went to the door and yelled up the stairs.

Danny took his time and it took another five minutes and two more yells up the stairs before a tousle-headed boy of around eight put in an appearance. Danny had stained shorts, scabby knees and a sulky expression.

'What do you want, Mum?' he demanded. 'I was playing on my computer.'

'It's not what I want, Dan. It's what these two policemen want.'

Danny turned sullen, dark eyes in their direction and said, 'Well? What do you want?'

Were kids scared of anybody these days, apart from the playground bully? Rafferty wondered. In his young days, two coppers appearing on the doorstep was an occasion of terror and the expectation of a good hiding. Not any more, it seemed.

'I wanted to ask you a few questions, Danny,' Rafferty replied. 'I understand you told Malcolm Forbes's men that you had seen the younger Jones boy climbing over the factory wall.'

'That's right. What of it?'

'I gather he climbs over the wall several times a day to save himself a walk?'

'Suppose. What of it?' he asked again.

'It's a high wall,' Rafferty reflected. 'Must be eight foot. I'd be hard pressed to get over it. How does he do it?'

'Brings a stepladder out from the house, doesn't he? His mum takes it back into the house after.'

'And what about from the factory side? Do you know how he gets over the wall from work?'

The boy shook his head. 'But it's a factory. There's probably loads of stuff lying around that he could use to climb over the wall.'

Rafferty nodded. 'I wondered if you'd noticed him do the same thing at other times?'

'I know what you're getting at. You mean like the day of the murder, don't you?'

'That's right. Did you see him climb the wall any time around three or a bit earlier that Friday?'

'Nah. I never saw him then.'

'You're sure? It could be important, Danny.'

'Course I'm sure. I'd have remembered if I'd seen him. He'd have been the chief suspect, wouldn't he?'

'Maybe. One of them, anyway.' Rafferty stood up. 'Thanks, Danny. You've been very helpful.'

Danny shrugged as if helping the police was all in a day's work to him. 'Can I go back to my computer game now?'

Rafferty nodded. As the boy rushed from the room, Rafferty

turned to Tracey and thanked her before he and Llewellyn left.

Billy Jones would still be at work at the factory. Rafferty didn't want to question the boy there and embarrass him in front of his workmates. He'd wait till Jones arrived home and question him there. Depending on what he said, they could check out his story with his supervisor later.

Meanwhile, the questioning in the neighbourhood was still on-going; there would be more statements to be read and digested, so they returned to the station.

Forensics' results on the mugging of Izzy Barber were waiting for them on their return. They'd come back more speedily than Rafferty had expected. Their results proved what he had hoped: Barber's blood had been found on two of the youths' trainers – those of Jake Sterling and Des Arnott. Let them try to 'no comment' their way out of that.

Billy Jones was at home when they called at the house at six o'clock. At first, he looked set to deny any wall-climbing activities, but then he seemed to change his mind and he admitted it.

'It's not a crime,' he told them forcefully, his ruddy complexion becoming a little redder as he said it.

'Not a crime, no,' Rafferty agreed. 'But for one thing, your employer might have something to say to you about your unconventional entries and exits from his premises. And for another, you are, of course, aware that we're investigating a murder. Don't you think your activities might have interested us?'

'I don't see why. Jaws was supposed to have been killed some time around three, as I understand it, and I was back at work by two. My time card will verify that if you want to check it.'

'Time cards can be punched by others, Mr Jones. And frequently are.'

'Well, mine wasn't. You can ask my supervisor if you want. He always stands by the clocking-in machine and makes sure no one clocks anyone else in. Nothing much gets past him.'

Rafferty nodded. 'I'll do that. Was there anything else you failed to tell us?'

'Like what?'

'I don't know. Anything you might have seen that will help us catch the killer.'

Billy Jones shook his head. 'I don't know nothing. Is that all?'

'Yes. That's all for now. But if your supervisor doesn't back up what you've said, I'll need to speak to you again.'

'He will. He'll tell you I was at work from two o'clock onwards.'

'We'll see ourselves out.'

Once beyond the gate, Rafferty said, 'We'll check with the supervisor in the morning. For now, let's call it a day. My stomach thinks my throat's been cut.'

Sixteen

The late Peter Allbright wasn't the only person to suffer despair. When Rafferty arrived home at eight o'clock that evening, he found Abra in similar straits, though from a different cause.

'My photographer rang me earlier. He told me he's double-booked for our day. He's got a big society wedding on the fourth Saturday in June. Guess who won his services? Not us, that's for sure. He can't even do the alternative date you said Father Kelly offered us. I've contacted every photographer in the area and none of them can do either day.'

'There must be one, surely? Are you certain you've tried them all?'

'Of course I'm sure. I've been through the Yellow Pages and not one of them can give me a firm booking. A couple said they'd put me in in case they had a cancellation, but that's not good enough. I want a firm booking for our big day. What are we going to do?' Abra was almost in tears. But then Rafferty had a brainwave. It was one that would require him to eat a considerable amount of humble pie, but the situation left him with no choice. 'Leave it with me. I think I might be able to come up with the goods.'

There was another disappointment awaiting him at the station when he arrived the next morning. Bill Beard hailed him as he came through the entrance doors.

'I've some bad news for you on the flower front. My auntie's had a stroke. It looks doubtful if she'll be doing much at all for the foreseeable future, certainly nothing so demanding of hand and eye coordination as making intricate bouquets and suchlike.'

'I'm sorry to hear about your aunt,' Rafferty commiserated.

Though not nearly as sorry as Abra was likely to be when he told her. Things were unravelling fast on his wedding plans. He only needed Llewellyn's mother-in-law to cry off from doing the cake and he'd be all but back to square one. The church and reception hall at least were organized. Father Kelly at St Boniface had been friends with his ma for years; she'd apparently had little trouble in sweet-talking the priest into providing the hall for nothing and the church and the organist for next to nothing. Father Kelly might even throw in the choir for a bottle of the hard stuff. He liked his tipple did Father Kelly. And just as long as he was sober on the day . . .

'Any chance of using one of her flower-arranging friends?' he asked. 'I know you mentioned they might be able to help out.'

'I don't know any of them and my aunt's not compos mentis enough to give anyone their names. No, I'm afraid it's back to the drawing board, Inspector. Hope it doesn't mean I won't get my invite.'

'Don't worry, Bill. You'll still get your invite. I'll see to it.'

He was weary of his attempts at wedding planning, most of which seemed to go awry no sooner had he thought something organized and fixed. He was back to square one with the flowers and had still failed to find a colleague ready, willing and able to let them have a free holiday home for their honeymoon.

However, he still had hopes on the flower front; for although Bill Beard's aunt was incapacitated, the wedding was still months off and there was time for her to regain her health. And even if her health was never fully restored, she should, within several months, have regained sufficient of her wits to let him have the names and phone numbers of some of her ex-florist friends whom he could suborn to get the job done.

Still, he felt sorry for the old lady. From what Beard had told him his aunt had been a doughty lady before her stroke. It was sad that she should have been struck down and left enfeebled. He had found out from Beard the name of the hospital ward and had sent her a get well card and a bouquet, half-hoping that the latter should be something less than expertly contrived so as to energize her brain and her critical faculties.

Of course, with neither flowers nor honeymoon organized, Abra was still plaguing him about both and doing her best to push her – more expensive, naturally – choices.

She still fancied a long-distance honeymoon destination, Goa or Bali being the current favourites, even though the latter had suffered bomb outrages in recent years. He was engaged in trying to persuade her of the charms of destinations nearer to home, such as France or Spain, which were the locations where those amongst his colleagues who had holiday homes had chosen to buy.

At the moment, he was working on Kenneth Drummond, the Uniformed inspector. Drummond was currently playing hard to get on the subject of letting him and Abra borrow his south of France holiday villa. But he hadn't said an outright 'no', so Rafferty was hopeful Drummond would give in if he kept up the pressure.

Distracted by the let-down over the flowers and the photographer, Rafferty wasn't concentrating too well. It was no good, he decided. He'd have to go out and get the job over. It was cowardly to leave it lying.

Nigel greeted Rafferty with a huge smile when he went to see him and explained his problem. It was a gloating smile and one that told Rafferty his cousin intended to extract as much satisfaction as he could from his dilemma.

'I thought you said you didn't want any favours from me?'

Rafferty squirmed and admitted, 'I know I did.' God, he thought, I'd give anything not to be put in this position. In spite of his cousin's handsome looks, Nigel gloating wasn't a pretty sight.

After several more minutes in similar vein, Nigel put his hands behind his immaculately groomed head and leaned back as if surveying a particularly pleasing sight before he admitted, 'I might be able to help you. Of course, you realize I'll have to charge you top whack.'

'And how much is top whack?'

Nigel named his price and Rafferty took a sharp breath

as he realized it was more than the most expensive quotation on Abra's list.

Nigel must have noted the look on Rafferty's too revealing face and said, 'Of course, I can lower the price for a consideration.'

'A consideration?' Rafferty's eyes narrowed suspiciously. 'What do you mean?'

'I'm still waiting for my invitation to the wedding, dear boy. An oversight, I'm sure.'

'Of course. It must have got lost in the post. I'll get Abra to send you a replacement.'

Nigel sat forward again. 'Then you've got a deal. You can have my man for your wedding day and I'll knock a hundred off the price.'

'Is that all?' It wasn't much considering he'd had to make the concession of inviting Nigel to the wedding. And it wasn't as if Nigel's man was a wedding professional. But as Nigel had made clear, beggars had to bite the bullet and accept what they could get. He didn't understand why Nigel was so keen on getting a wedding invitation. Perhaps he only wanted an opportunity to sneer? He just hoped Abra never learned that the man who was to capture their wedding for posterity photographed houses for a living.

After his humbling brainwave on the photographer front, driving back to the station another brainwave came to him. He told Llewellyn about it as soon as he got back to the office.

'We already know there was collusion between the residents indebted to Forbes. They agreed to lie about not seeing Harrison on the afternoon he was murdered But what if they colluded *before* his death?'

'What? All of them? Old Emily Parker and the two young women, too? Surely not!'

'A collusion too far, you think?'

'I'd say so.'

Rafferty grunted. 'Maybe you're right. It was just an idea.'

'Not one that runs, I wouldn't think.'

'Try this one for size then. I had another idea. Well, actually, I put two unconnected thoughts together. I might have come out with five. Tell me what you think. Tracey Stubbs was described as a bit of a goer by Tony Moran. Clearly, with three kids and another on the way – and all by different fathers according to the gossip on the street – she's no Virgin Mary.'

'Go on.'

'Well, I was wondering if one of her kids might not be by Jaws Harrison and—'

'Jaws Harrison? Why would he have anything to do with Ms Stubbs? It's not as if she's in debt to Forbes and—'

'And decided to pay him in kind? No. I know that. Not now, she's not. But maybe she took out a loan from him earlier and paid it off.'

'I still don't see what it could have to do with the murder even if she did have a previous loan. Surely it's the here and now with which we should be concerned.'

Rafferty wasn't entirely sure himself where he was going with this one, but he persevered. 'Maybe he encouraged her to pay him in kind a few times and she fell pregnant by him?'

'And she decided to get her revenge?'

Rafferty nodded.

Llewellyn looked sceptical, as well he might. Rafferty realized that he should have thought about this longer and deeper before he'd revealed his thoughts in the cold light of day and to Llewellyn's even colder logic.

'She's almost due to have her baby,' Llewellyn pointed out. 'If that's the one John Harrison is meant to have fathered. Any attack can hardly have been prompted by a murderous rage about his impregnating her, if that's what you're implying. She's had nine months to take her revenge.'

Rafferty wasn't sure what he was implying. 'I know that, as a theory, it's got a few flaws in it,' he admitted. 'But I think I'm on to something.' It was clear that Llewellyn didn't agree with him. But although he said nothing further, Rafferty had a feeling he *was* on to something. He just wished he knew what. Frustrated, he said, 'Let's get over to the factory and speak to Billy Jones's supervisor.'

Before they went into the factory, Rafferty poked his head around the corner of the building and saw how Jones had managed to climb the high wall. Leaning drunkenly against it was a pile of sturdy wooden palettes which would make climbing the eight-foot wall easy. Once on top all he would have to do was ease himself down by his hands and drop a couple of feet.

The supervisor, a Mr Simpson, confirmed what Jones Junior had said and handed over his time card. The card agreed with what both Jones and Simpson had said. So that was that. Another possible trail come to a dead end.

Rafferty, determined to get *something* else organized on the wedding front, went and saw Nigel again before he tried any other avenues in the investigation. Having had no joy amongst his colleagues for a cost-free honeymoon, he turned again to his last resort. His cousin Nigel had just returned from what, to judge by his tight waistband, had been a very good lunch. He was in a mellow mood and greeted Rafferty in a jocular manner.

'Oh, look,' he said to no one in particular, 'it's the poor relation come to beg for more scraps from the rich cousin's table. Shame I didn't ask the waiter for a doggie bag.'

'I've had my lunch, thank you, Nigel. I came to see you about something else.'

'Oh, yes? And what might that be?'

Rafferty didn't beat about the bush. 'Seeing as we're back in the business of giving and receiving family favours, how are you fixed for lending us a holiday home?'

'A holiday home? This'll be for the honeymoon, I take it?' asked Nigel.

'That's right. I wondered if you might have branched out into foreign lets and sales.'

'As a matter of fact, I have. It's another new venture. It's not been going long, but it's doing well.'

'I'm looking for a nice villa in the south of France. At special family rates, of course.'

Nigel smiled. 'I'm surprised you're asking me. Surely some of your overpaid police colleagues have a holiday home or two between them?'

'Never mix business and pleasure. That's always been my motto.' In truth, he'd have been willing enough to mix the two if only one of his colleagues had cooperated, it being preferable to get a free loan of a holiday let for the honeymoon than pay out whatever Nigel thought reasonable. Unfortunately, Kenneth Drummond, the colleague he had most recently tried to talk into the rental, had turned him down flat after playing with him for several days. 'Perhaps you can let me have a brochure?'

'Certainly.' Nigel whipped a colour brochure out of his desk drawer. 'And seeing as you'll be renting in June before the holiday season gets into full swing, I can give you a ten per cent discount on the usual price. Most of my clients would be glad enough to get a two-week booking at a time they'd normally expect their places to be empty not to quibble about the price reduction.' He nodded at the brochure. 'You and Abra have a look through that and let me know your choice and I'll get it booked for you.'

Rafferty hefted the brochure. 'Thanks, Nigel. I'll get back to you once we've had a look through this.'

'You do that. I shall want a ten per cent deposit, of course. Cash will be fine.'

I'll bet, thought Rafferty. What was Nigel up to? Was he letting his clients' property on the side and pocketing the money? He wouldn't put it past him. And who would be any the wiser, as long as the clients didn't turn up at their holiday home out of the blue and find, like Father Bear in the nursery rhyme, that someone had been sleeping in *their* bed.

Rafferty, not wanting to have his and Abra's honeymoon ruined by owners turning up unexpectedly, said, 'I hope this is kosher, Nigel. Abra would never forgive me if we were turfed out of our honeymoon villa in the middle of the night by the arrival of irate owners.'

'You worry too much. It'll never happen. Trust me.'

It was clear Nigel wasn't worried. But then it wouldn't be his honeymoon that was ruined. He probably already had his excuses ready in case the owner found out. An oversight. A misfiled booking. A genuine error of some sort. Nigel would wriggle out of it somehow and if the worst happened he'd lose a client, whereas Rafferty would lose a good start to his married life and give Abra a stick to beat him with for ever. But, he reasoned, if Nigel could take a chance so could he. A ten per cent reduction on the price wasn't to be sneezed at. And at least it would be one more thing on his list organized.

Abra had the holiday brochures out and spread all over the coffee table and settee when Rafferty arrived home. She was surrounded by them, each cover destination looked more exotic and costly than the previous one.

'You can put those away, sweetheart,' Rafferty told her as he flung his coat over the back of the settee and flourished Nigel's brochure. 'I got us a good deal on a villa in the south of France.'

'The south of France? But I fancied somewhere more far-flung for our honeymoon.'

'There's nothing wrong with the south of France. And do you really want to spend the best part of a day either way scrunched up in an airplane seat when we might be enjoying our own pool and celebratory champers?'

'Well, when you put it like that . . .'

'You know it makes sense.' Rafferty, sensing he was on a winning argument, pushed it onwards. 'We'll have a look through this brochure after dinner and choose somewhere nice.'

Abra glanced at the cover of the brochure and pursed her lips. 'Don't tell me that's Nigel's firm?'

'The very same. That's why I got a good deal. It's all kosher,' he quickly assured her, crossing his fingers behind his back. 'And there are some lovely places in here. And won't it be good to get our honeymoon sorted?'

Abra still looked doubtful. 'Nigel, though. You know what a double-dealing, underhand so-and-so he can be. Are you sure he won't cheat you?'

'He'd better not. I'm a policeman. No, even Nigel knows better than to cheat the law. He might be a ducker and diver, but he's not daft.'

'I'll get dinner dished up.' Abra crawled from under the pile of brochures, tidied them into a neat heap and went into the kitchen.

After dinner, they settled down together on the settee and went through Nigel's brochure.

'There are some lovely places in here,' Abra commented. 'Look at that one. It's got a huge swimming pool, a barbeque pit and a spa. That'll do for me. It's a short distance from the nearest town, too, so we could walk in of an evening for dinner.'

Rafferty was more than happy to fall in with Abra's choice. They cheerfully made plans for the rest of the evening and went to bed early.

'To get in practice for the honeymoon,' as Rafferty jokingly told her.

By the time he woke the next morning, Rafferty was convinced there must be something he'd missed on the investigation. Was it something someone had said during the course of the interviews? He didn't know. When he got into the station, he and Llewellyn went through all the statements and discussed every personality right from the beginning of the case. But nothing struck him.

It was only when they'd got to the end of this mammoth task that he began to get another idea. It was the merest glimmer of an idea and might come to nothing, but he thought he knew just the person most likely to have information to help the glimmer grow: Mrs Emily Parker, the woman who was forever in and out of the houses of her neighbours and, like Ma, knew more about each of them than they knew themselves. If anyone could tell him what he wanted to know, she could.

'Turned up out of the blue she did one day. As I said, I'd never seen her before so it made me curious. Anyway, next time she came calling I was in my garden and made sure to catch her when she came out. I invited her in on some pretext or other and she was happy enough to agree. It didn't take long to get her story out of her.' Emily Parker sat back with a smile. 'I'm a good listener. Anyone will tell you.'

Rafferty didn't doubt it. He'd been hoping and praying that her ferreting skills were an equal to her listening ones. And so they'd proved to be. He thanked her for her time and the information she had so willingly provided and headed for the car. What she had told him gelled with one or two of his own ideas. All he had to do now was check them out. In pursuit of this, he climbed in the car and headed across town.

Seventeen

'I know who killed Jaws Harrison,' Rafferty announced triumphantly as he came through his office doorway. 'I even know why and what was the murder weapon. It wasn't a hammer, which Sam Dally thought a possibility. It was a metal-tipped walking stick.'

'You mean Jim Jenkins? He's the only one to my knowledge who uses one. I recall it was unusual, being all metal rather than wood.'

Rafferty nodded.

'So why did he do it?'

'You remember the first time we called round to his house and his granddaughter was there?'

'Yes. A pleasant young woman. Mr Jenkins seemed very fond of her.'

'He is. Very fond. But I only found out how much when I decided to pay another visit to Emily Parker, the proverbial nosey neighbour, to see what she could tell me about the girl. She'd seen Kim visiting him and was naturally curious because there had never been any sign of the girl until two years ago and Mrs Parker's lived beside Jim Jenkins for years. She tried to get the information out of Jenkins without success, him being the taciturn sort, so, unbeknownst to Jenkins, she waylaid the girl one day when she'd been visiting, plied her with tea and biscuits and found out the relationship. Young Kim's apparently a bit artless and was clearly putty to an experienced information gatherer like Emily Parker. Anyway, I went round to see the girl and she admitted to me that she was in debt to Malcolm Forbes.'

'But she wasn't on the list that Forbes gave us. There was no Kim on it.'

'There wouldn't be. It was her grandfather's pet name for

her. He was fond of Kipling's *Jungle Book* and called her
Kim from that. She was adopted as a baby – her real name's
Alicia West.'

'West. The list of debtors is alphabetical. We hadn't got
as far as the Ws.'

'She checked out her parentage when she reached the age
of eighteen and got to know her grandfather soon after. I
think he was bitterly ashamed that he'd made his daughter
give the baby up for adoption – she stayed with an aunt in
Liverpool for six months which is how Mrs Parker didn't
know of the pregnancy. Young Kim, or Alicia – whatever
you want to call her – said her grandfather had admitted as
much. He was sorry about all the years when they hadn't
known one another. It made him even more protective than
he might otherwise have been. So when Jaws started threatening her for non-payment and her grandfather got it out of
her, he decided to kill the man who had frightened her. I
gather that Jaws, apart from the threats, had also more than
intimated that she could pay him in kind.

'I checked with the Royal Marines, which was the lot he
was with in the war, and Jim Jenkins had been a commando.
Well used to killing by stealth, even if he's crippled with
arthritis now. I doubt if Jaws Harrison even heard him come
up behind him.'

'Have you spoken to Mr Jenkins?'

Rafferty shook his head. 'I couldn't. He's been admitted
to hospital and isn't expected to live. He's got advanced
prostate cancer with secondaries. But he left me a letter
which he dictated to one of the nurses in which he confessed
to what he'd done and why he did it.'

'Killing Harrison wouldn't have helped his granddaughter
for much more than a week or two.'

'No. He realized that. But he thought the man deserved
to die. And so he killed him. He has some savings which
he's already given to Kim with the proviso that she pay
Forbes off. And she and her natural mother will share the
money from the sale of the house between them so she should
never get into debt with someone like Forbes again.'

'Why couldn't he just give her the money to pay off Forbes
in the first place rather than kill Harrison?'

'As I said, Jaws had made a play for the girl suggesting she could pay him in kind next time she didn't have the money. Jim Jenkins thought redemption was in order. I suppose with his old army training killing was the regular habit for doing away with enemies. That's why he targeted Harrison rather than Forbes himself. Who can blame him? It's not as if Jaws Harrison is any great loss to the world.'

Rafferty made for the door. 'I'm off to see the super.'

'Hoping for another pat on the head?'

'Certainly am. And why not? Case over.'

Epilogue

The murder was solved, as were the muggings. And now, apart from the wedding flowers which were back in his bailiwick again, there only remained one job for Rafferty to do – sort out his best man for the wedding.

He'd finally decided on Llewellyn. He was certain he'd do a much better job than either of his brothers or any of his friends.

'Ah, Daff,' he said when Llewellyn came back from fetching the morning tea. 'There's something I want to ask you. I've been putting it off because I've had so many other things on my mind, but I was always going to ask you.'

'Ask me what?'

'Will you be my best man?'

Llewellyn smiled. 'I thought you'd never ask. Of course I will. I'll be delighted.' His smile deflated. 'Only you might change your mind when you hear my confession.'

'Confession? Not another one.'

'Not to murder. Just to telling Maureen one or two things I perhaps shouldn't have done.'

'Like what?'

'Like that I did the invitations for your wedding. And that Nigel Blythe's house photographer is booked to take the photos.'

Rafferty beamed. 'No harm done. I'm sure Mo can keep a still tongue in her—' He broke off, dismayed. 'I see. That's it, isn't it? She couldn't keep a still tongue. Don't tell me she's told Abra?'

'I'm afraid so. I've just had Maureen on the phone. She thought she ought to warn me. And you.'

'How did Abra take it?'

'Like she was on the warpath and with the tomahawk aimed at your head.'

Rafferty slumped in his chair and slurped some of his consoling tea. 'I suppose that means the wedding's off.'

'It certainly will be if she catches you. Maybe you ought to stay at my place for a night or two until she cools down.'

Rafferty, recalling how caught up in the roar of the wedding Abra had been lately, said, 'A week or two might be better.'

The phone rang just then. It was Abra. Rafferty's ears began to ring.